BARBARIAN

EMPIRE
BOOK 2

PENELOPE SKY

HARTWICK PUBLISHING

Hartwick Publishing

Barbarian

Copyright © 2023 by Penelope Sky

All rights reserved.

No part of this book may be reproduced in any form or by any electronic or mechanical means, including information storage and retrieval systems, without written permission from the author, except for the use of brief quotations in a book review.

CONTENTS

1. Bartholomew — 1
2. Laura — 7
3. Bartholomew — 15
4. Laura — 23
5. Bartholomew — 35
6. Laura — 43
7. Bartholomew — 47
8. Laura — 57
9. Bartholomew — 63
10. Laura — 67
11. Bartholomew — 83
12. Laura — 95
13. Bartholomew — 113
14. Laura — 119
15. Bartholomew — 143
16. Laura — 153
17. Bartholomew — 173
18. Laura — 185
19. Bartholomew — 195
20. Laura — 211
21. Bartholomew — 225
22. Laura — 233
23. Bartholomew — 243
24. Laura — 251
25. Bartholomew — 257
26. Bartholomew — 285
27. Laura — 295

28. Bartholomew 315
29. Laura 321
30. Laura 327
   Epilogue 343

1

BARTHOLOMEW

I sat in the waiting room, my arm wrapped in a tight gauze. My jacket was bloodied and ruined, so I'd shoved it in a garbage can after I got Laura into the hands of the doctors. Now I sat there, the TV in the corner showing the twenty-four-hour news cycle, an older couple in the opposite corner, eyeing me warily from time to time— like they knew I was bad news.

I *was* bad news.

Bleu entered the room then slowly approached me.

I wasn't in the mood to talk, but I couldn't ignore my responsibilities. "How many men did we lose?"

"Two."

"Who?"

Bleu sat beside me. "Hector and John."

It could have been worse, but it was still a stinging blow. "And how many did they lose?"

"A lot."

"Leonardo?"

"He survived. I think a bullet grazed his leg."

Bastard.

Bleu glanced at my arm but didn't ask if I was okay. "What are your orders?"

For the first time in my life, I didn't have any.

"We have to retaliate."

I couldn't. We made a deal—and I was a man of my word. "There will be no retaliation."

Bleu turned his head to look at me. "They opened fire when we left."

"He never guaranteed our safety."

Bleu always followed orders and kept his head down. Did as he was told. But not today. "We can't let him get away with this—"

"Bleu." My head rested against the back wall, and I turned my head slightly to look at him. "You think I give a shit about anything right now? Until she gets out of surgery, I'm mentally incapacitated."

Bleu had a flash in his eyes, an urge to argue, but he made the wise decision of keeping his mouth shut. "I'll wait for your call." He left the waiting room.

The couple left too. Must have overheard our conversation.

Now I sat there alone.

Minutes later, someone else joined me.

"Where is she?" He surveyed the sea of chairs, as if she'd be sitting there. He came over to me, frantic gaze, his body clean like he'd scrubbed all the blood and dirt away before he came here. "The lady at the desk said she was in surgery—"

"That's where she is. In surgery."

Victor gave a heavy sigh before he dragged his fingers down his face. "Is she going to be okay?"

"She's tough. She'll be fine."

"The doctor told you that?" he asked hopefully.

"I'm telling you that."

He stood near my chair, still upset because that reassurance wasn't enough. "Is there internal bleeding? Did the bullet hit an artery or an organ?"

"The surgery is to remove the bullet."

He gave a sigh of relief. "Okay…that's pretty routine."

"Why are you here?"

"For Laura—"

"If you really give a shit about her, you'd kill Leonardo with your bare hands."

His face turned as pale as fresh milk. "I had no idea—"

"I'm sure nobody did." Leonardo had fattened her up like a pig for slaughter. Told nobody that he intended to turn her into bacon. Couldn't risk it getting back to her. Because if it did, she'd take Victor's gun and shoot him in the back of the head. "You want to keep working for a man like that? I've been called a madman, but that man is truly psychotic. There are lines you don't cross—and that's one of them."

"I-I don't know."

My eyes narrowed. *"You don't know?* Your wife was raped, and you did nothing about it. Here we are seven years later, and now she's been shot in the arm by your boss, and again, you do nothing."

"It's complicated—"

"It's not complicated at all." I was on my feet, my voice louder than the TV in the corner, ready to tear through my stitches as I beat him so bloody he would be the one in need of surgery. I moved forward and he moved back, his eyes locked on mine. "You have no right to be here. Leave."

"I need to make sure she's okay—"

"*Leave.*" I stepped closer to him, got right in his face, just seconds away from grabbing him by the neck and slamming his face into the wooden arm of a chair.

Like the pussy he was, he fled.

2

LAURA

My consciousness stirred slowly. It started off as a faded dream. Then my thoughts formed. They were incoherent at first, but then they started to solidify, and I started to remember things.

Like being shot in the arm...by my father.

My eyes opened, and I gasped in terror.

He was there, his hand on mine, sitting right at my bedside like he'd been there the entire time. Dark hair. Dark eyes. His calm command soothed my terror as his thumb stroked my hand. "You're in the hospital. You had surgery to remove the bullet from your arm. The doctor said you'll be fine."

I looked down at my arm, seeing that it was wrapped up in a sling. I moved my fingers then tried to lift my arm, but it hurt like a bitch, so I stopped.

"You'll have to wear that for a couple days."

"I don't have a couple days."

"You need to rest—"

"No. I need to get a gun and shoot that motherfucker twenty times in the face! Now get this shit off me."

"Laura—"

"Nurse!" I had an IV stuck in my arm and other wires connected to my body. I was basically a prisoner in this goddamn bed. "*Nurse!*"

"Laura." He got to his feet then gently pressed me against the bed, getting me to lie back again. "Revenge can wait. Right now, you need to rest."

"Rest, my ass."

He kept his hand on my shoulder, so I was stuck in place. His eyes dared me to fight him.

Now that I was stuck there with no one to shoot in the face, I felt it—the excruciating pain. The pain meds must have worn off, and maybe that was why I'd woken up. I looked down at my arm again, remembering the moment I'd been shot, the blood that immediately soaked the sleeve of my sweater. I remembered the cold metal against my scalp, the kiss from the barrel of his gun. My rage was tempered by my pain—both physical and emotional.

Bartholomew returned to his seat.

When I looked at him, I realized I wasn't the only one hurt. "Are you okay?"

"I'm fine." He crossed one ankle over the opposite knee and sat there, his eyes bloodshot and tired like he'd been awake for days. "A bullet grazed me. Just needed a couple stitches."

"I'm sorry." It must have happened when he carried me to the car.

"It's been a while since I've been shot anyway. I was due." His humor was drier than stale bread.

I looked out the window, the plastic blinds closed, little cracks showing the daylight outside. With the adrenaline and rage gone, I was left with a distinct emptiness. I'd betrayed the person at my bedside for someone who didn't hesitate to shoot me. When I told my father everything, he immediately schemed this entire plot. "He knew I wouldn't be able to persuade you..." He'd known how it would end. Me on my knees—his gun to my head. And he would keep shooting me until he got what he wanted. I could have bled out and died. He could have hit an artery. I could be dead right now—and he didn't care.

My own father...didn't care whether I lived or died.

A day later, I was discharged from the hospital, my arm still in the sling.

Bartholomew must have made an arrangement with Victor, because my belongings had been returned to me. Instead of taking me to his place in Florence, we went straight to the airport and flew back to Paris.

He was attentive but also quiet, barely saying more than a couple words to me.

So deep in my sadness, I didn't feel like talking much anyway.

We returned to Paris, and his driver took me to my apartment. Bartholomew grabbed my bags and carried them inside.

It'd been so long since I'd been there that it felt like a foreign place. My computer was still on the dining table. The dirty dishes in the sink had been washed and put away. A vase of fresh flowers had been placed on the counter. The bowl on my kitchen island now held an assortment of fresh fruit.

He must have had one of his guys break in to my apartment and stock it.

I felt violated and touched at the same time.

Once Bartholomew put my luggage away, he joined me in the entryway. "Do you need anything?"

The question took me by surprise because I'd assumed he would stay. To do what exactly, I wasn't sure. But I didn't expect him to drop me off and then walk out. "No..."

"Call me if you need something." He moved to the door and prepared to leave.

"Bartholomew?"

He turned back around. His look was like concrete—hard and lifeless.

"You can stay..."

His gaze remained empty. He was neither sad nor angry. There was nothing behind those beautiful eyes. "No, I can't."

My eyes darted to different places because I didn't know where to look. Heat seared the backs of my eyes and down my throat. I could feel the moisture grow deep in my eyes, feel the drops form but remain locked under the surface. "Look—"

"Let's have this conversation when you're feeling better."

Fuck. "I'm not going to feel better for a long time." I was traumatized by more than the bullet. I was traumatized by how horrible people really were. I'd never been truly loved by anyone in my life—except my mother. "I wish I could take it back—"

"But you can't."

"I'm so sorry..."

"I know you are."

"Please—"

"Laura." His voice was like a knife through soft bread. "Two of my men were killed. I know your father finds everyone expendable, but I don't. I'm as loyal to my men as they are to me. I destroyed their trust when I forfeited everything to save you. My flawless reputation now has a mark I can never erase."

I was so fucked. "You didn't have to save me…"

His eyes narrowed in their angry way. "I would never let anything happen to you. Even if you weren't loyal to me—I'm always loyal to you."

This hurt so fucking bad. "Bartholomew—"

"You made your choice. You have to live with those consequences."

I blinked and did my best to restrain the tears.

"My offer still stands. I'm here if you need me." He turned to the door and walked out.

I watched him shut the door and leave.

And then I cried.

3

BARTHOLOMEW

For the first time in my life, I was ashamed.

Too ashamed to return to the Catacombs and show my face to my men.

They followed my orders because they believed in me. Served me like soldiers protected their king. But I'd turned my back on them—*for a woman*.

I sat at the bar by myself, mixing pills with alcohol, indifferent to the damage I was doing to my liver.

A couple people looked at me, as if they knew I didn't belong there. Some women gave me attention, but they seemed too intimidated to approach. The chairs on either side of me stayed vacant because no one wanted to be near me.

Finally, someone was brave enough to take a seat.

Benton.

He tapped his fingers on the counter and got his drink.

He was the last person I expected. I continued to drink and look straight ahead, not in the mood for company, not even from him.

"Bleu told me what happened."

"I assumed."

"How's your arm?"

I swirled my glass and took a drink. "I wish it hurt more. I'd welcome the distraction."

Benton took a drink.

I looked into the bottom of my glass. "You don't have to do this."

"Do what?"

I took a drink. "I know you want nothing to do with me, Benton." Our last conversation had blown up into an angry fight. We hadn't spoken since. I wondered if we would ever speak again. "I want your friendship—not your pity."

"My anger doesn't change our relationship."

"It should." I'd never felt this level of self-loathing.

We sat in silence. Glasses lightly tapped against the surface of the wood. Quiet conversations in various languages continued throughout the quiet bar. There was no music.

"How's Laura?"

"She'll be fine." She'll have an ugly scar for the rest of her life, to match the one on my stomach.

"You ended things."

It wasn't a question, so I didn't answer. Just let the truth of his statement reverberate. "I'm so fucked, Benton." There was just ice in the bottom of my glass, so I shook it around just to listen to the sound. "I lost two guys when I should have lost none. My men watched me sacrifice everything for a goddamn woman." I grabbed the glass and threw it at the mirror in front of me. It shattered into pieces, and everyone turned silent. The bartender stilled. It took a couple seconds for people to start talking again. I tapped my fingers on the counter as I stared at the frightened bartender. "Another."

He made the drink as quickly as he could, pouring some of the booze on the counter instead of in the glass. He slid it to me and took off to find something else to do—far away from me.

Benton was the only one unfazed by my outburst. "Why did you save her?"

I drank from my glass and let the silence linger.

"She chose them over you. You didn't owe her anything."

"I know."

"You really think he would have killed her?"

I stared into my glass as I remembered the scene, the edge in Leonardo's eyes. "Yes."

Benton stared at the side of my face. "A father kill his daughter?" he asked, slightly incredulous.

"He was that desperate." It was the only card he had left. "If he didn't, I would have taken everything. His wealth. His respect. Everything that matters to him. His estranged daughter that disapproves of his life...not nearly as important." My parents had abandoned me and started a new life with their new kids, and watching Laura be abandoned by her father...it stung. I wouldn't wish that betrayal on anyone. It was the kind of hurt that went so deep you couldn't cut it out, not with a knife, not with therapy. "He wouldn't have shot her in the head, but in her arms and legs until I caved or she bled out."

"Jesus."

"Claire is lucky to have you, Benton." Luckier than the rest of us.

"You can't forgive her?"

I took another drink. "No."

"You wouldn't have saved her if you didn't care about her."

"Never said I didn't."

"Maybe—"

"It's done. I won't change my mind." The only thing that mattered in life was loyalty—and she pissed all over it. "Now I have to move forward…but I'm not sure how."

"You can start by killing him."

"If that were an option, I wouldn't be sitting here talking to you." I'd hang him from the Duomo so everyone could see his body at first light, a broken neck and a stiff body.

"I agreed not to return there in exchange for Laura. And if I don't keep my word, then my tarnished reputation will be rusted."

Benton turned quiet.

I drank.

He drank.

There wasn't anything left to say.

"I'm sorry," he said finally. "But the men will forgive you."

"They shouldn't."

"You made a mistake."

"But it wasn't a mistake. Just as Laura made her decision, I made mine. It was intentional. It's unforgivable."

"A father was about to kill his daughter," he said. "They probably felt for her."

"John and Hector are dead."

"They knew the risks. They all do."

I appreciated Benton trying to make me feel better, but nothing would heal this wound. "I'll have to earn their respect again—assuming they don't stage a coup and slit my fucking throat while I sleep."

"They won't do that, Bartholomew."

"Really? Because that's exactly what I would do."

4

LAURA

A week had come and gone.

The sling finally came off, but it was still hard to move my arm. The muscles were stiff with trauma, but my doctor told me to use it as normally as possible so it would rehabilitate. If it didn't get better, I'd have to try physical therapy.

I didn't hear from Bartholomew—and I knew I would never hear from him again.

The heartbreak hurt a lot more than the bullet.

I worked to keep my mind occupied, to stop thinking about my insatiable need for revenge and my all-consuming heartbreak. I pushed through the pain because I had to get better. Had to get my strength back.

Because that was the only way I would be able to kill my father.

I sat alone in my apartment, holding a bag of ice to my arm because it hurt after a long day of moving clothes and delivering suits to residences. My apartment was silent. My laptop screen had gone black because it'd been idle for so long. I hadn't had dinner yet, but I would probably skip it because my appetite was nonexistent.

All I could think about was one thing.

Bartholomew.

I fucked up so bad.

I knew I couldn't fix it.

But I missed him…so much.

In my desperation, I texted him. *Can you come by?*

I didn't expect a response. He said he would help me if I needed assistance, but stopping by for a late-night chat didn't fall under that offer. I didn't want to pretend I needed help either, because that would be a lie, and I respected him too much to do that.

His response was nearly instantaneous. *Be there in 10 mins.*

My heart did a weird flip and a somersault. I felt lighter than air. But then it came crashing down a moment later, dropping into my stomach and a pool of acid. Now I was nervous, cold and clammy, terrified. This all happened in the span of five seconds.

Exactly ten minutes later, he knocked on the door.

God, I was going to be sick.

I opened the door and came face-to-face with those dark eyes. They were the color of coffee but didn't have the warmth of a fresh brew. His jawline was covered with a thick shadow that was almost a beard. He gave me the same look as the last time I saw him—of pure nothingness.

I was too speechless to invite him inside, so he let himself in.

He took a look around as if he expected to see the source of my call. As if there was something broken for him to fix or something too heavy for me to move with a single arm. When he saw there was nothing, he looked at me again. "What do you need?" His voice was deep like velvet, strong with confidence, innately powerful.

The sight of him made me weak because he was so damn handsome. I missed the nights when he showed up on my doorstep just to fuck me on the kitchen counter or in the shower. He wasn't one of those guys that was insistent on leaving the second the fun was over. He slept beside me and kissed my naked body in the morning. "I just wanted to talk."

His eyes locked on mine, a hint of anger on the surface. "I told you to call me if you needed help."

"You told me to call if I needed something—and what I need is to talk to you."

The anger deepened as he stood there. Several seconds of silence passed. "Fine." He moved to the round kitchen table, sitting in the chair he used to occupy when we had dinner together. He was in his signature leather jacket and boots.

I took a seat across from him, nervous under his piercing stare.

"Let's get this over with."

With an attitude like that, I wasn't going to make any progress. This conversation was pointless. "How's your arm?"

His hardness decreased, but only slightly. "It's fine."

"Did they take out the stitches?"

"They dissolved."

"So, your arm is back to normal—"

"My arm is fine, Laura." He looked out the open window. "How's yours?"

I hated it when he called me Laura. I missed sweetheart. "It's really stiff. The doctor said I should use it as much as possible to get it back to normal."

"Good advice."

"I'm not looking forward to having a scar."

"A scar is better than death." He turned his head and looked at me again. His muscular arms stretched the fabric of his jacket in the sexiest way. His broad shoulders blocked out the chair that supported his back. He'd always been irresistible, but he was even more irresistible now that I couldn't have him.

"You're right."

Silence spread between us, the air becoming more tense as the time passed.

He stared at me, waiting for more.

"I miss you…" I didn't know where to start, how to begin, so I just spoke from the heart.

He didn't react. Didn't even blink.

"I wish...I wish I could take it all back."

"But you can't. Just as I can't take back the betrayal to my men."

"Bartholomew—"

"You've been estranged from your father for seven years. *Seven*. But you didn't hesitate to turn your back on me for him. I killed the men who touched you. I broke Lucas just for trying to touch you. I was loyal to you—to the death."

"I know—"

"I haven't even spoken to my men yet because I don't have the balls to look them in the eye right now." He raised his voice. "Never in my life have I been ashamed, but I'm fucking ashamed." He leaned over the table, coming closer to me, jabbing his finger into the surface. "I don't know what's going to happen when I walk in there. They might burn me alive and spit on my body. Wouldn't blame them if they did."

"You didn't have to save me—"

"I don't regret my decision, Laura. I would have saved you a hundred times—because I actually care about you."

"I shouldn't have gone to my father. I shouldn't have been so stupid, and trust me, I will regret that for the rest of my life. But let's not forget that you lied to me, Bartholomew."

He leaned back in his chair.

"You walked into my shop with the intention of using me."

"Then I changed my mind—"

"But the foundation of our relationship was a lie. You didn't walk in there because you wanted to fuck me. You walked in there because you wanted to use me as bait. And then you kept that secret to yourself for *months*."

He hadn't blinked in nearly two minutes. "You made it very clear this wasn't a serious relationship, so I wasn't required to tell you."

"What did you expect me to do when I found out? Do you have any idea what kind of situation you put me in?" Now we were yelling back and forth at each other, our voices shaking the walls of my apartment.

"I sure as fuck didn't expect you to dump me and go to your father. Nor did I expect you to tell him everything. Not after I'd proven to you what kind of man I was. Maybe I should have told you the truth, but you shouldn't have chosen him."

"You think I don't know that?" I asked, my voice cracking. My eyes watered, hot with angry tears. "I will kill that man before this is over. I will shoot him over and over until he bleeds out on his favorite rug."

He wore a hard stare, like he shared no delight in that ending.

"Please…give me another chance."

I was barely holding it together, and he looked devoid of all emotion. "Laura, I told you I wouldn't change my mind about your father. Not for you. Not for anyone. The same thing applies to this. I won't change my mind."

It was a knife to the stomach. "Bartholomew—"

"You're the one who ended this relationship. Remember that."

"Because I was angry—"

"And if your father hadn't been a piece of shit, you wouldn't be asking me to take you back."

"We don't know that—"

"You want me back because I took bullets for you. You want me back because I gave up *everything* for you. You want me back because you've finally realized you're the one who's not good enough for me." He got to his feet so quickly the chair went flying back.

I got up too. "I've never thought that I was better than you—"

He headed to the door but then stopped abruptly to look at me. "You said you didn't want to date someone like me—"

"After the shootout that injured us both, I think that's pretty fair."

"I wanted to be your man, but you didn't want me to be."

"I just didn't want anything serious—"

"Because I wasn't good enough for you." His eyes were furious. "That's why, Laura. I was only good enough to be your secret fuck buddy. I was only good enough for hotel rooms and shadows. You went on a date with some other guy because I wasn't worthy of that respect."

"I didn't go on a date—"

"It's more than just picking your father. It's everything. And believe it or not, I deserve better than that."

Ouch. "Bartholomew, my mother was murdered and I was raped—"

"And when your father turned on you, who was the one who saved you?"

I turned silent.

"I promised I wouldn't let anything happen to you and I kept my word, so I'm sick of hearing that excuse."

The tears escaped my eyes and came pouring down. "I don't want you back because I want us to keep sleeping together. I don't want the relationship we had before. I want something more. I want...whatever you're willing to give me."

His hostile stare wasn't penetrated by my tears.

"I don't care what you do for a living. I don't care about the risk. You're what I want... I'm sorry it took all this to make me realize that. Don't ever think you aren't good enough for me, Bartholomew. You're...the first man who's ever made me feel safe."

His look hadn't changed. "It's too late, Laura."

"It's never too late."

"I've already slept around."

"I don't believe that." I knew he was a cold man, but I didn't believe I had been miserable for the last week while he'd felt nothing at all. I refused to believe he'd slept with strangers while I slept alone. "You wouldn't do that."

He turned to the door and walked out.

No.

"Don't call me unless you actually need something." He said the words with his back to me as he walked down the hallway. "Otherwise, I'll stop coming."

5

BARTHOLOMEW

The vehicle stopped beneath the bridge.

Headlights went out. Engine went cold.

"Time to face the music, huh?" Like the coward I was, I hadn't shown my face for a week. Production continued without a hiccup, so that gave me hope I hadn't completely fallen from grace. "What can I expect?"

"Some of the men are angry," Bleu said from beside me.

I gave a slight nod.

"But some know you didn't have another choice."

I didn't deserve the rationale. "Alright." I opened the door, and we entered the hidden entrance to the Catacombs. The place was dark and dank, but I felt the drop in energy the second I stepped inside. The men I passed stared at me, not in reverence or respect, but in the way you looked at an animal that just got hit by a car. You knew it was going to die in the next few minutes, and you wondered if you should just put it out of its misery now.

It was a long walk of shame, taking the winding passages lit by torches. The deeper inside I moved, the staler the air became. The dead stared back at me, and I wondered how fitting it would be if they added my skull to the collection.

After what felt like an eternity, I entered the cavern where we all gathered. The men drank at the tables, and all the conversation immediately died away once I joined them. It was so quiet, the sound of my boots echoed against the ceiling that was fifty feet in the air. My chair sat there, unoccupied, not appropriated like I feared it might be.

I could feel the collection of emotions throughout the room. Hatred. Betrayal. Pity.

Shit I hated.

All eyes were on me, so it was time to address the men who'd blindly followed me for so long. "I'm not one for words, so let's cut the shit. I fucked up—and I fucked up bad. I won't apologize, because an apology is a request for forgiveness, and I don't deserve forgiveness. I won't explain my actions because an explanation doesn't justify the outcome. My only hope is we can move forward."

"And move against the Skull King?" Silas sat on one of the benches, leaning forward with his elbows on the table, asking a question when he already had the answer. It was a provocation, an attempt at humiliation, forcing me to tell everyone in the room that I was a goddamn pussy.

"I gave my word I wouldn't retaliate. And you know a man is only as good as his word."

Silas stared me down, like hearing my answer angered him more. "That's how you do Hector and John? They died for you—and you won't even avenge them?"

"It's not that I don't want to—"

"But you won't."

I'd already lost considerable power because men usually didn't speak to me that way, and if one of them did, my men would snap his neck without waiting for me to give the order. I was entirely on my own. "I gave my word."

"Well, you gave us your word too. Look how that turned out."

I held his gaze, keeping calm and bottling my frustration. "I've led the Chasseurs for a decade. In that time, our presence has grown to exceptional heights. We've taken Croatia as well as France. We have so much power that we're untouchable by both the government and the police. In fact, we're in bed with both of them. Our profits are immense, and I've always passed those profits on to you instead of keeping them all for myself. An error in judgment doesn't dismantle all the victories that got us here. I ask you to remember that before you cast your prejudice."

It was silent.

My words seemed to have an effect.

Well, except on Silas, who continued to look at me like I was rotten meat.

"Are you okay?"

I stared across the room, watching everyone mingle with drinks in hand, some of them oblivious to the paramount corruption right under their noses. The leaders of our country couldn't care less about the drugs on the street—as long as they were taking a cut.

A hand moved to my shoulder. "Bartholomew?"

My head snapped in her direction the second her fingers made contact with my jacket.

She flinched at the ire in my eyes.

I didn't like to be touched.

She pulled her hand away. "Guess you answered my question…"

I looked away and didn't ask for elaboration.

"You seem angry."

"I'm always angry."

"Angrier than usual."

Because I was.

"Is it about that girl?"

"Woman." I didn't fuck girls.

"I'll take that as a yes."

I drank from the champagne glass and cringed—because champagne tasted like piss.

"What happened?"

"She betrayed me."

"How?"

I stayed quiet because I didn't want to talk about it.

"Was there someone else?"

"No."

"Then how did she betray you?"

I was growing tired of bringing Camille to these things. Now she felt comfortable questioning me about shit that was none of her business, and she was becoming noticeably pregnant, so that wasn't great for my image. I told her the story in as few sentences as possible.

For once, Camille was shocked into silence.

"It's over."

"Don't you think you're being a little unfair?"

"No."

"You do realize that situation never would have happened if you hadn't slept with her, right? Once you knew you didn't need her, you could have just walked away. But you didn't. You're solely responsible for the situation she was in. You dragged her into it."

I looked elsewhere, ignoring her face.

"You're being a little harsh."

"She made her choice, Camille."

"So, she was supposed to not care that you were going to destroy her family?" she asked incredulously. "It's not just her father, but her sister, her other relatives tied up in the business. You just expected her to blindly choose you? What are you, a narcissist?"

"Yes, but that's not the point."

"Bartholomew—"

"Your opinion means nothing to me."

That shut her up.

I'd had to grow eyes in the back of my head because a number of my men were no longer loyal to me. At some point, there would be an attempt on my life. My work had been my home, but now I had to look over my shoulder every second of every day when I walked through the front door.

"I can tell you're miserable without her."

"I'm miserable because she ruined my fucking life."

"Just—"

"*Enough.*" I looked her dead in the eye, and my threat was unmistakable.

That was the end of the conversation—and probably the end of our business relationship.

6

LAURA

I was sitting at the table with my laptop and a glass of wine when someone knocked on the door.

My eyes flicked up immediately, and my heart gave a lunge.

What if it was him?

He was the only person who stopped by my apartment unannounced. And it was evening, just before he started his day. I looked like hell with my hair in a bun and my face without makeup, but that wouldn't stop me from opening the door.

I looked through the peephole first—and my disappointment fell to the floor like a heavy brick.

It was Victor.

The second I opened the door, he looked me over with concern, like I'd still be bleeding a week later. "I had to see that you're okay."

I didn't have the energy to argue, so I walked back to the table and dropped into the chair.

He joined me, taking Bartholomew's seat.

It hurt to look across the table and see anybody but him.

Victor continued to stare at me with hesitancy. "So...are you okay?"

I took a drink of my wine. "Physically, yes."

He eyed my right arm, where the nasty scar was visible. It was black and blue because the bruising would be there for several weeks at least. "I had no idea, Laura."

"I know."

"If I did...I would have shot him."

I wasn't sure if I believed that. He talked the talk, but he never walked the walk, not like Bartholomew.

"He asked me to come up here."

My eyes narrowed. "He could have called."

"He knew you wouldn't answer. And if he came in the flesh…he wasn't sure what would happen."

Because he's a fucking coward. "Now that you've seen me, you can head home."

He remained motionless. "Are you still with him?"

I wanted to lie, but I couldn't bring myself to do it. "No."

Victor's eyes gave a subtle flash.

"He dumped me…and I don't blame him."

Victor watched me. "He should have told you the truth."

"Maybe. But I shouldn't have picked my psychotic father who couldn't care less about me instead of the man who actually did care about me." I couldn't take it back now. I was alone, and being alone never bothered me until now. I felt vulnerable and exposed. I felt like I'd had a lottery ticket in my hand, and I'd let it slip away in the breeze.

"Bartholomew is a bad guy, Laura. It may not seem like it right now, but this is a blessing."

"No. Leonardo *is* a bad guy. Bartholomew is a fucking saint compared to him."

"He deals with some rough characters."

"He killed the men who hurt me…and I didn't even have to ask him."

Victor's eyes dropped momentarily, full of shame.

We sat in silence for a long time.

"Would you be willing to talk to him?" Victor asked.

"Who?"

"Your father."

"Do I really need to answer that?"

He looked away again.

"I never want to hear his voice or see his face again. Make sure he knows that."

He gave a subtle nod.

I'd lived in this world long enough to know what was really going on. My father was gathering information under the guise of remorse, trying to figure out if Bartholomew was still in my life and if I was intent on revenge. Because if I did intend to kill him, I had the strongest ally in the world.

But I decided to give him a false sense of security instead.

7

BARTHOLOMEW

I walked through the parlor and took a seat on the leather armchair.

Armando and his brother were waiting for me, ready to get down to business.

The liquor was poured. Short pleasantries were exchanged.

I had to keep my eye on my men as well as theirs now.

"We can't sell this amount of supply within the timetable you've given us," Armando said. "We were told we would have more customers, but that didn't work out."

I would suffer this humiliation for a long time. "I just met with the prime minister. We should be able to cross our northern border into Belgium without being searched soon enough."

Armando kept a straight face, but I could tell he was impressed.

I had to improvise if I wanted to stay on my feet, if I wanted to keep the respect I'd worked my ass off for.

Then Bleu stepped into the room and locked eyes with me.

As if he had something he needed to tell me.

"Excuse me." I left the sitting room, and Bleu and I entered a different parlor. "What is it?"

"Victor came to visit Laura."

My eyes narrowed the second I heard the name of that coward. "Alone?"

"Yes."

"Did she let him in?"

"Yes. He hasn't left."

A tightness formed in my chest, like a cord being wrapped around my body. "How long has he been there?"

"An hour."

"You're certain he came alone?"

"We've checked all the streets in a one-mile radius. Haven't seen anyone who shouldn't be there."

Leonardo would be stupid to come to my territory because then he would be fair game. So he sent Victor—his bitch—to do his work. And Victor was probably too stupid to realize he was an expendable pawn on our chessboard. "Tell me when he's gone."

I knocked on her door and waited.

Her feet shuffled on the other side. A shadow formed over the peephole. Then she knew it was me.

She opened the door, her eyes wide with surprise because she probably thought she'd never see me again. Her hair was in a loose bun at the top of her head, showing off her slender neck. Her face was free of makeup, but her eyes were still stunning.

The last thing I wanted to do was give her false hope. I wasn't cruel. "What did he want?"

Her entire face deflated like a balloon popped by a tiny needle. It was slow...and agonizing. "You're still watching my apartment."

"If your father steps foot into my territory, the truce is void."

Once she understood my motivation, her skin went pale as chalk.

"What did he want?" I repeated.

"To see if I was okay." Her voice was quiet, as if she barely had the energy to string a couple words together.

"What else? He was here for an hour and seventeen minutes."

Her stare hardened, but she still didn't have the energy to get angry. "What does it matter?"

"Trust me, it matters. Now, answer my question."

"He asked if we were still together...and I said no. He said my father wanted to call, but he knew I wouldn't answer. I told Victor that Leonardo better stay away from me. And that was it."

"He's putting out feelers."

"I know. That's why I tried to throw him off the scent... even though I'm coming for him." She reached for her arm and lightly massaged it. "Once my arm fully heals, at least." She walked back to the table and took a seat.

There was nothing left for me to do but leave.

"Sit with me." She refilled her wineglass. "I have a proposition for you."

I studied her for a while before I dropped into the chair across from her, the place I assumed Victor had just occupied. My anger throbbed underneath the surface, annoyed that he had the audacity to come here and act like he gave a damn.

"What?"

My eyes flicked to hers.

"You look angry all of a sudden."

"I don't think Victor had any business being here."

Her fingers rested on the stem of her glass. "He said he didn't know my father's plan. I believe him."

I believed him too. But that didn't change anything. "Your proposition?"

She rebuffed my coldness by taking a drink. "We both want him dead. Let's work together." Her face glowed with sincerity. She had the tint of blood lust in the corners of her eyes. The same rampant rage I felt bottled in my chest was bottled in hers. It wasn't an empty threat, but a true motivation. She'd had a week to cool her temper, but now she glowed red like she'd been roasting above a campfire that entire time.

I'd never found her more beautiful. "Sparing his business was the condition of your release."

"But not sparing his life."

"I vowed not to return to his territory."

"Then we'll lure him out of that territory."

"I appreciate your enthusiasm, but he's not an idiot."

"I told him we weren't together anymore. So you could threaten to kill me unless he comes to Paris."

I didn't want to remind her why that wouldn't work, but she left me no choice. "He would have kept shooting you until I caved. He was fully prepared to kill you, Laura. So, no, that plan won't work."

Her eyes were shielded, so whatever hurt she felt deep inside was invisible. "He didn't play by the rules, so why do you?"

"Because I'm a man and he's a coward." Simple as that.

"Look." She moved her glass to the side so she could put her hands on the table. "I'm going to kill this asshole whether you help me or not. But I'd prefer it if you did. We both want the same thing."

Hearing her talk like that sent a series of flashbacks across my mind. "I can't."

"Is your word really that important?"

"My word is everything. It's the foundation of my business relationships. It's the foundation of my reputation. My men want to retaliate, but I also had to tell them no. You have no idea how hard it is for me to sit here and do nothing." I struggled to express my anger with words. I preferred violence.

She went silent, realizing there was no way to convince me. Her eyes were down on the table.

My eyes were on her face.

She finally straightened and sat back. "Then I'll do it by myself."

I didn't think that was a good idea either, but it wasn't my place to tell her what to do. "Be careful. Remember, if it comes down to you or him, he's going to choose him." And I wouldn't be there to protect her.

"Trust me, I know." She looked out the window, the city lights bright on the road outside her apartment. "I'm going to take his business too. And once I do, I'm going to give it to you on a silver fucking platter."

My eyes narrowed.

She met my gaze, the determination burning in her eyes. "It belongs to you, Bartholomew. You earned it fair and square—and I screwed it up. I'm going to make this right."

"Laura." I kept my voice steady. "I sacrificed everything to keep you alive—and I want you to stay alive. More money and more territory…it's nothing compared to you." Her blood lust was sexy, but the risk to her safety was not.

She stared at me for a long time, her eyes immobile, not blinking. "I knew you were lying."

Her accusation made my mind go blank because I had no idea what she was referring to.

"You aren't sleeping with anyone else. There hasn't been anyone but me."

My face was hard as stone. I'd had years to perfect the coldness.

"Bartholomew—"

"I'm not doing this again. And please don't kill your father and steal his business because you think it'll get me back. That won't work either."

She wrapped her arms around herself and pulled one knee to her chest. She regarded me across the table like she was seeing me with a fresh pair of eyes. "You can't treat your personal relationships the way you treat your business relationships."

"That's exactly how I should treat them. If you can't trust your partner, they shouldn't be your partner. And I don't trust you."

Her eyes immediately closed, like those words packed a punch that knocked her teeth out. When she opened her eyes, she looked out the window.

"I feel like I'm back in time."

After a pause, she looked at me again.

"She chose her family over me. Never looked back."

Her eyes started to shine with a reflection.

"She married someone else. You will too. I just hope he's more interesting than an accountant."

The tears in her eyes pooled to drops, but she closed her eyelids to keep them contained. After a few seconds of silence, she opened them again, somehow holding the tears behind her lashes. "Don't be cruel."

"Cruelty is all I know."

8

LAURA

Another week passed.

The only thing that consoled my heartbreak was my desire for revenge. I fantasized about it, imagining how I would make my father pay for what he did to me. I would punish him for hurting me. I would punish him for what happened to my mother.

My arm looked better, but it still stung with pain when I did too much. I wouldn't be able to throw a punch. It was my dominant hand, so it would be hard to stab someone too. But I also knew I couldn't just march up to my father and shoot him at point-blank range.

No, that wouldn't work.

I didn't want to shoot him and walk away.

I wanted to make him hurt.

I wanted him to feel *betrayed*.

Countless times, I considered going to Bartholomew's apartment and saying something that would change his mind. But that man was as impenetrable as concrete. It didn't matter that his feelings for me hadn't changed.

He was the most stubborn man I'd ever met.

If his ex hadn't hurt him so deeply, I might have had a chance…but she fucked it up.

I fucked it up.

I collected my bags then stepped outside into the warm air. It was summer now and the air was hot and humid, and my body instantly started to sweat under my blouse.

I stood at the curb and waited for my ride to show up, and that was when my phone rang.

Bartholomew.

The second I read his name, a lump formed in my throat. I feared the day I wouldn't see that name anymore, when he stopped watching my apartment because he didn't care about me anymore.

I answered. "Hey."

"Laura." His voice was stern, like a parent scolding a child. "Get your ass back on the plane."

I missed him, even when he was pissed off at me. "No."

"Don't do this."

"I have to."

"Laura, it's not worth it. Live your life—and live it well."

"I can't." My father didn't just break my heart. He ruined the best relationship I'd ever had. I think I hated him more for that than shooting me. "I have to do this."

"You have no chance. He'll finish the job."

"I have a plan—"

"An idiotic one. All of this is idiotic. I sacrificed my reputation so you would live, not go back into the lion's den." He sounded so angry, I imagined him storming around his apartment throwing his arms about, knocking over lamps because he was so irate. "Get your ass back on the fucking plane—"

"If you care about me this much, then why won't you forgive me?"

Silence.

"Give me another chance if you're this upset." I'd never begged for a guy. Never chased a guy. But I knew he was the only one I wanted, and I believed there was still hope. He said one thing, but the heart on his sleeve was a direct contradiction.

"Are you playing me right now?" Now his voice was quiet—but ice-cold. "Thought if you took a plane to Italy you would force my hand?"

"No—"

"That shit isn't going to work."

"That's not what I'm doing—"

"Bullshit," he snapped. "How stupid do you think I am?"

"I was just pointing it out—"

"I don't want you, Laura. The second you stabbed me in the back, I despised you. Is that what you want to hear from me? I deserve a woman who judges me based on who I am, not what I do. You never appreciated me."

I disagreed, but there was no point in making an argument. "Goodbye, Bartholomew." I hung up the phone, knowing I had to sever contact. Otherwise, I'd start sobbing right there on the sidewalk with tons of people around.

I took a breath then looked at my phone, seeing that the driver was still five minutes away. I just wanted to go to my hotel and lie in bed…and cry until I fell asleep.

Minutes later, my phone started to ring again.

It was him.

I was so upset, I almost didn't answer.

Almost.

I took the call but didn't say anything.

When he spoke, his voice was calm. "I can't protect you this time, Laura."

"I never expected you to."

"I broke my word for you once, and I won't do it again."

"I know."

He stayed quiet on the phone for a long time. There was nothing left to say, but he didn't want to hang up. "Be careful."

9

BARTHOLOMEW

I sat in the armchair in the parlor, in my sweatpants and nothing else. The phone was gripped tight in my hand, the corner of the metal resting against the side of my face. Footsteps sounded behind me.

"Bartholomew?"

I stared out the windows to see the city in daylight. I'd been home for hours, but I was too worked up to sleep. When I looked in the mirror, my eyes were bloodshot like I used the drugs I pushed on the streets.

Bleu came into the room and looked directly at me. "Is this a bad time?"

Every moment of every fucking day was a bad time. "What did you discover?"

He hesitated, and that told me it was bad news. "The guys are pretty guarded toward me. They know I'm loyal to you."

I stared out the window again. I had to double the security around me at all times, even though it wouldn't make much difference. The men who wanted to kill me could be the ones put on guard to protect me. I had to be prepared for war at any moment. Guns were tucked in hiding places throughout my home. I slept with an assault rifle beside me instead of a woman. "I'll speak to him privately."

"You think that's a good idea?"

I looked at him.

Bleu immediately dropped his gaze, knowing he'd said the wrong thing.

"I need you to do something for me."

"Yes?"

"I need you to send a few men to Florence."

His eyebrows immediately rose. "You've changed your mind."

"No. I need them to tail Laura day and night—and make sure they aren't seen."

Bleu wore the same incredulous look on his face.

"We've got to put our best guys on this. Leonardo will use his own men to follow her, so they can't suspect anything."

His arms crossed over his chest. "I'm not sure if any of the men will agree to this."

"Not all of them hate me."

"It doesn't exactly look good, that you're willing to send men to protect a woman, but not send men to scout—"

"Just make it happen, Bleu."

10

LAURA

I walked up to the iron gates of my father's estate.

The security guys stared at me like they couldn't believe I'd returned. They made their calls on their radios, and then the gates opened so I could pass. But they conducted a thorough search.

And I mean thorough.

They patted down my breasts, checked my bra for a knife stashed in the fabric, felt my entire pelvis, not just my ass.

"Do I look like a hooker to you?" I smacked one of them when he slid his hand right over my crotch.

Then they made me walk through a metal detector.

I cast them a glare once I finished. "Was the pat-down really necessary, then?" I walked up the steps to the front door, and the butler was there to greet me. He was wary around me, like his neck was on the line.

I wasn't like my father. I didn't kill innocent people. "I want to see him."

"He'll be with you shortly. Let's go into the parlor." He took me into the room where I'd spoken with him many times. He let me take a seat before he exited the room.

I sat in the armchair alone, combing over everything in the room, tempted to look for weapons he'd stashed. I knew they were everywhere. When I was a child, I was told I'd get a horrible beating if I touched any gun that I found. They were strapped underneath tables, on the backs of dressers, hooked behind TVs on the wall.

I wondered if there was one in that very room.

Someone entered the room—but it wasn't my father.

It was Victor.

His face was strained, and his eyes were annoyed, like he wasn't happy that I was there. "Laura." He came close and sat in the other armchair. "What are you doing here?"

"I want to talk to him."

"Why?"

"Because he *shot* me. Why else?"

"I-I just assumed you wouldn't come back. You said you didn't want to hear from him ever again."

"Well, I'm still really pissed off, and I want the opportunity to tell him how pissed off I am. And that motherfucker is going to sit there and listen to every goddamn word I have to say." I lifted my arm. "Look at this."

His eyes stayed on mine.

"*Look.*"

He dropped his gaze and looked at the horrible scar.

"That's why I'm here."

My father entered the room, wearing a sport coat despite the unbearable heat outside. His eyes locked on mine.

Mine locked on his.

It was a silent standoff, both of us testing the other, the silence growing in intensity with every second that passed. Victor left the room without being dismissed, and then it was just the two of us.

My father studied me from the door, keeping the space between us, as if he didn't know how to approach me.

As if he was afraid of me.

As he should be.

He finally entered the room, choosing the chair Victor had just vacated.

The rage was indescribable. It was hard to look at his face and just sit there instead of getting out a knife and slicing his nose clean off. The blood boiled in my veins, the pressure so great, they were about to pop. It took all my strength to maintain a calm composure, to stay in my chair instead of launching myself right at him. "Fuck. You." It was all I could manage. The only coherent thing I could get out.

He took it with indifference, as if he'd expected this reaction.

"You...fucking...shot me." It was hard to get the words out, because every time I spoke a syllable, I was brought back to that night when the barrel of the gun was pressed right to my skull. It was cold as ice.

"Laura—"

"Your *daughter*." My eyes filled with tears, angry ones. "How could you do that to me?"

His eyes shifted away.

Good. He had no right to look at me.

"I had no other option—"

"There's *always* another option. You could have killed me."

"I was careful with my aim—"

"And what if Bartholomew didn't cave? You would have just kept shooting me?"

"Of course not." He looked at me again. "I knew he would cave."

I didn't believe him. Not one bit.

"And I had to make it look real. I had to convince him I wasn't bluffing."

And you weren't.

"I-I can't believe you didn't tell me."

"It had to look real, Laura."

"But you planned to use me as a pawn that entire time. You knew I wouldn't be able to convince him."

"A man like him isn't going to be persuaded by a woman's pleas."

God, I was so stupid.

"I understand you're angry, Laura—"

"Angry doesn't even begin to describe it. I told you everything…and you treated me like a dog."

"There was no other way. Bartholomew had me pinned down. It was either that—or lose everything. Laura, you saved our family. You saved our legacy. I hope you understand the sacrifice you made."

"But it wasn't a sacrifice—because it wasn't my choice."

His gaze hardened. "He would have killed all of us."

"Only if you didn't cooperate."

"And you think I'd submit?" he asked incredulously. "You think I'd ever take orders from someone else? You think I'd ever be someone else's bitch? Yes, I'd rather die—and he already knows that."

I didn't want my father to end up like that, refusing to cooperate and getting shot in the head. If that did happen, I'd probably never want to speak to Bartholomew again. Regardless of what I decided, Bartholomew and I would be apart right now.

But in this scenario, I looked like the bad guy.

It could have easily been him.

That was the moment I stopped feeling so terrible about my betrayal. If I hadn't betrayed him, he would have betrayed me. When I'd begged him to stop this, he could have backed off, and we'd be in Paris right now...my ankles locked around his waist.

My father's voice brought me back to the conversation. "You saved us, Laura. And for that, I'll be eternally grateful."

His pretty words would never sway me. I wouldn't be gaslit, not this time.

"I hope you understand how sorry I am. How horrible I felt in the moment."

I couldn't accept his apology so easily. That would be suspicious as hell. "I'm relieved no one got hurt but me. I'm relieved that the livelihood of our family is preserved. But I don't forgive you."

His eyes shifted back and forth between mine, and he actually looked hurt. "Are you still seeing him?" He already had that information from Victor, but he asked me anyway, just to be sure.

"No. He couldn't look past my betrayal."

"You protected your family. He would have done the same."

Not Bartholomew. "I miss him, but…it is what it is."

"He wasn't the right man for you, Laura. The only interest he had in you was your connection to me."

And that bit him in the ass. If he hadn't walked into my shop, his plan would have been successful. He should have just walked away, and after getting my heart broken, I wished he'd done exactly that.

"I see the way Victor looks at you."

My eyes locked on his.

"There's been no one serious since you."

My face remained indifferent, but a seed was planted—by my own enemy.

"Just thought you should know that."

Victor was waiting by the entryway so he would see me when I left. He was in a black t-shirt with dark jeans, the normal shadow on his jawline now a short beard. His dark eyes locked on me the second I came around the corner. He even looked me up and down, as if to make sure I was unharmed.

I walked up to him. "Let's get lunch."

He stilled at the invitation, his eyes shifting back and forth quickly, as if he couldn't believe what I'd just said. "Alright."

We left the estate together and walked down one of the side streets until we found a café. It had paninis and pastries with espresso, so we ordered a couple things and took a seat.

Victor looked out of place, like he felt he didn't belong there...or with me.

I took a drink of my espresso, getting the caffeine kick almost immediately. My heart didn't race the way it had before when I'd come face-to-face with my father. I was still angry, angry enough to kill, but the rage was tempered as I began to lay out my plans.

"Are things good between you?"

Not even close. "He made his argument. Total bullshit."

Victor didn't touch his coffee or sandwich. He'd probably already eaten lunch but didn't want to pass up the opportunity to see me one-on-one. "Then you're going back to Paris." His disappointment was palpable.

"Actually, no."

His eyes narrowed.

"I'm definitely staying. I've got work to do, and you're going to help me."

Victor's confusion intensified, his handsome face becoming sterner. "Help you what?"

"Get my revenge."

His muscles stiffened noticeably, and his confidence started to wane. "Laura—"

"This is what we're going to do. He's going to think we've gotten back together. We'll have to take our time with this to make it believable."

His eyebrows furrowed as he listened to me.

"You're going to help me earn his trust. Let his guard down. Return to his inner circle."

"Why—"

"Because I want him to hurt the way he hurt me. Because I want the emotional scar to be more painful than the physical one. Because I want him to feel as small as he made me feel when he shot me in the fucking arm." I didn't keep my voice down. Couldn't care less if anyone overheard me. I was certain the locals weren't oblivious to the Skull King and his illegal activities.

Victor's eyes flew back and forth between mine. "When he finds out, he'll kill me."

"No, he won't."

"If he shot you in the arm, he'd have no problem shooting me between the eyes."

"He won't shoot you because he'll be dead."

Victor turned silent.

"By my hand."

"Laura, I understand you're upset—"

"Victor, I could have just pretended to want you and accomplish my goals that way, but I respect you too much to lie to you. You're going to do this because you owe me—and you owe me big."

His gaze relocated elsewhere, like he was trying to figure out how to get out of this.

"You should want him dead after what he did to me."

"Who says I don't?" His eyes came back to me. "But you don't understand how powerful he is. You don't understand how far he can reach. He's been the Skull King for a long time, and he has a lot of men in the palm of his hand."

"Once he's dead, you think they're going to come after me?" I asked incredulously. "All they're going to care about is taking his spot. You think they'll give a shit that his daughter hated him so much she shot him? It's a family matter, not a business one."

"If you want to kill him, just take a gun and shoot him."

"He expects that, so it won't hurt. He has to trust me. He has to think I'm his loyal daughter."

Victor took a deep breath then scratched his beard as he considered it. "I thought about killing him myself. When I witnessed what he did to you...I could no longer see him the same way. He had the others watch me, like he thought I might retaliate. It hasn't been said out loud, but I know he lost the respect of some of his men when he shot his own daughter. Family is the most important thing in our culture, and he shit all over that." His arms crossed over his chest, and his food remained untouched. "I'm willing to do this for you—but it's still a lot to ask. I'm putting myself at risk, and your father is one of the smartest men I've ever met. He's not exactly easy to cross."

I felt like there was more, so I stayed quiet.

"So I want something in return."

"You want something in return?" I asked with a light laugh.

"I could just slip poison into his scotch. Could stab him in his parlor and walk straight out the door. But this plan is far riskier. So if you want me to do it your way, you need to make it worth my while."

"What do you want, Victor?"

He stared for a long time.

I knew where this was going.

"I want another chance."

"Another chance to what?" I played dumb, hoping he would back off.

"Another chance to be with you. I'm not the man I used to be. I've proven that by agreeing to help you."

"If you were the man you should be, you would kill him because he deserves it."

"I'll go kill him right now—but it's not the way you want him to die. And I know you want to be the one to pull the trigger."

I felt the intensity of his stare, knew how angry Bartholomew would be if he heard this conversation—even though he would have no right to be angry. "I'm not ready to move on, Victor. Bartholomew and I just split up a couple weeks ago. It's too soon." I couldn't imagine another man's lips on mine. Couldn't imagine someone else in my bed. Couldn't picture anyone but Bartholomew.

Victor seemed unsurprised by this. "Then when the time is right, I want the opportunity."

"Victor." I didn't understand his ongoing affection. "It would be easier for you to find someone else and start new. With us...we're always going to be living in the past. It's not as if you can't have any woman you want."

He didn't say anything to that, like he needed time to form a response. "That's true. But you're the woman I love."

I couldn't meet his stare. "I don't know how you can say that when you're the one who asked for the divorce."

"I didn't ask for it because I didn't love you. I just… couldn't handle what happened."

"Well, what happened has still happened. I was raped, Victor. I will always be a woman who was raped. If we sleep together, all you'll think about are the men who forced themselves on me. Nothing has changed—just the date."

He didn't flinch when I said all of that. "That's not how I see you, Laura. I thought that before because I was a boy. But now I'm a man, and I see you as you are—a strong and beautiful woman."

I was the one to look away.

"It hurt to let you go. It wasn't like I just forgot what we had. Years passed, women came and went, but I never forgot you. I think we've been given another chance to be together—and we should take it."

"The only reason we have a chance is because Uncle Tony died, my father shot me, and my boyfriend dumped me. How romantic."

"You know that relationship had no future. It was based on lies. His lies."

I still didn't look at him, thinking about the man who had ripped my heart out of my chest. There was no scenario in which that relationship would have lasted, but I still felt like I'd lost the best thing that ever happened to me. It hurt more than when Victor asked for a divorce. "Maybe that's true…but I'm still heartbroken, nonetheless."

Victor studied me for a long time, swallowing my confession with a stern face. "Are we in agreement?"

His question brought me back to the conversation. "Yes."

The second he got the answer he wanted, his eyes softened a bit, like he'd just proposed and I said yes.

11

BARTHOLOMEW

I sat at a table in the museum, a drink in my hand, listening to my world come crumbling down.

"The Prime Minister of Belgium has determined the substances have come from our border. In order to remain cooperative, I have to increase border restrictions. I'm sorry, Bartholomew."

"We had a deal." The room was full of obnoxious people in obnoxious suits, and I had the prime minister's full attention because I knew all his dirty secrets. I knew about the prostitute he'd knocked up. She had the kid, and now he was paying her every month to keep her mouth shut. His wife had no idea—for now.

"But you decided not to be discreet and flooded the market with more product than they could handle. I'm not to blame for this."

"Don't add the restrictions."

"If I don't, I'll look complacent."

"You *are* complacent, Prime Minister." And not just because he'd fucked a whore without a condom. He was guilty of other shit, like money laundering and extortion. My old friend Fender had shared the goods. "If you won't open the borders, then you need to find an alternative route, perhaps the train system."

"That train is for passengers."

"The cargo is irrelevant."

Frustrated, he looked away, watching the other people in the room mingle. His own wife chatted with their eldest daughter, a girl who had just started university. What would she think if she knew she had a one-year-old baby sister? "My hands are tied—"

"The only way your hands are tied is if I tied the rope. And right now, your hands are free."

He continued to look away.

"Figure it out. Or you know what the consequences will be."

I headed across town, and the driver dropped me off in front of the bar. It was a quiet night, few people on the street and even fewer people inside. Some of the tables were occupied, and light music played overhead. A couple TVs in the corners showed the twenty-four-hour news cycle.

I spotted Silas across the room, sitting at a table with a couple guys I didn't know. They were drinking beer on tap—like pussies. I visited the bar first and grabbed my drink before I took my time crossing the room, making eye contact with Silas before I arrived.

He held my stare with a stone-cold expression.

I took a drink, my eyes locked on him.

Once the guys recognized the tension, they looked at me over their shoulders.

My eyes were reserved for Silas.

He finally dismissed his guys with a subtle head nod.

When they took his silent order and disbanded, I realized this man had a life outside of the Chasseurs.

I took an unoccupied seat across from him.

He stared.

I stared.

A silent standoff.

He took a drink.

I did the same.

He eventually crossed his arms over his chest and sank back into the chair.

"We need to bury this," I said.

"We do?" he asked, cocking his head to the side.

"We do if you want to remain in the Chasseurs."

"You're threatening me, Bartholomew?"

"You've seen me threaten people, Silas. That's not what I'm doing—yet." I knew this fucker hated me. I knew this fucker was the most likely to stage a coup. "Air your grievances so we can move forward."

"You want to hear my grievances?" he asked with a slight laugh. "You're a pussy. That's my grievance."

I kept up my hard stare.

"We had that asshole by the dick, and you forfeited all of it—to get your dick wet."

My dick had been bone-dry.

"John and Hector. Dead. Because of you." He sat forward slightly. "I might be able to tolerate you if you got off your ass and avenged our guys. If you avenged our reputation. But you sit there…like a goddamn pussy."

"Enough with that word. We both pay good money for pussy, so it's not a bad thing. It's a lazy insult."

His eyebrows furrowed.

"I think we can both agree that pussy is life."

His gaze remained hard.

"I fucked up, Silas. I'm not going to justify my mistake. I'm not going to pretend it's okay. I regret what happened, and I wish it had been different. But I've led us to countless victories this last decade. The Chasseurs were just a concept before I took over. I've turned our hustle into a billion-euro enterprise. I can confidently say I'm the only one who could pull that off. So let's accept this loss as a wash and move on."

"You're the one who said a lifetime of loyalty doesn't justify a single betrayal."

"It wasn't a betrayal."

"That's not how we see it."

We? "An innocent woman would have died—"

"So?" he snapped. "You should have let her die."

Even if I could go back and do it all again, the outcome would have been exactly the same.

"We should be in Italy right now, guns blazing."

"I told you we can't do that—"

"And that's why you're going to end up in an oil drum."

My expression hadn't changed, but everything in my body contracted with enough tension to launch me onto the roof. My own men had never threatened me, but now the promise of violence was laid out on the table.

He waited for a reaction, but he got nothing out of me. "You can't kill me, Bartholomew. Because if you do, you know what will happen."

The men would turn on me. Right now, the atmosphere was mostly civil. People were slowly forgetting what happened in Florence and moving on. But if I killed Silas...one of my own...they wouldn't trust me. It didn't matter that he threatened to kill me, not when I deserved it. "Don't fuck with me, Silas."

He grinned at me. "You know what? A month ago, I would have taken a bullet for you. I would have gone to any lengths to serve the enigmatic and powerful Bartholomew. But now...I don't respect you. You have no business leading us. You forfeited that right the second you refused to get your hands dirty. Stepping down would be the honorable thing to do...but you aren't honorable."

"Dinner is ready, sir."

I walked straight past my butler like he wasn't there.

"Would you like to take it in the dining room—"

A large vase was on one of the entryway tables, decorative crap that the designer had picked out when I bought the place. I grabbed the table and pushed it over, sending everything to the floor, where it crashed into a million pieces.

Then I kept going.

He didn't ask me about dinner again.

I made my way upstairs to my bedroom, stripped off my jacket and tossed it on the floor, and then headed straight to my private bar. I finished my drink before I threw the glass against the wall.

It shattered like the vase.

My phone vibrated with a call from Bleu.

I ignored it.

I took a shower, skipped the shave, and then stepped into the bedroom with just a towel around my waist.

My phone lit up, and I had four missed calls from Bleu.

Must be important. Silas probably rallied the guys together to chop off my head or run me out of Paris.

I finally answered. "What is it, Bleu?"

"I just got a report from the guys in Florence. Thought you'd want to know."

I couldn't believe I still worried for her—after she fucked me over like this. "Is she okay?" I hated asking the question. I hated caring.

"She's fine. Visited the family estate."

"Is she staying?"

"She rented an apartment, so I'd say yes."

So, she was going through with her idiotic plan.

"But there's something else."

"Yes?"

"She's spending extensive time with Victor."

I stilled when I heard that fucker's name.

"They've had dinner together a couple times."

My jaw was clenched so tightly I was about to grind my teeth into dust.

"Do you have any orders?"

Shoot him in the back of the head—and make her watch.
"No."

"How did it go with Silas?"

"He threatened to stuff me in an oil drum."

Bleu said nothing.

"So, it was a good day…"

I walked into the Underground and headed straight for the office in the rear.

Jerome barely had the chance to turn and look at me before I dropped the wad of bills on his desk. "Brunette with big tits. Now."

Jerome couldn't take his eyes off the cash for several seconds. That was the kind of payment for an entire month of entertainment, but I'd just dropped it for a single night, for a woman with the kind of magical pussy that would make me stop thinking about someone else. "Give me a couple minutes."

I waited in the bar, sitting there alone as I waited for what I paid for.

Thirty minutes later, he presented a woman who fit my description, with brightly colored eyes and an enthusiasm that seemed genuine. She looked me over like she couldn't believe she got paid a fortune to screw a man she'd probably fuck for free. "I'm Serenity."

I didn't bother telling her my name. "Let's get out of here."

I took her to a hotel because I didn't want my place to smell like anyone else but me. I stripped off my jacket and yanked my shirt over my head once we were in the room. Then I took a seat on the couch with my arms sprawled over the back of the couch.

Serenity began her seduction dance, slowly peeling off her clothing, taking her time unzipping her dress before she stepped out of it and worked her bra.

My eyes were fixed on her, but I couldn't see her.

I saw a different brunette.

I saw eyes both kind and vicious.

I saw a woman who had been beaten by the world but refused to cower.

Flashbacks came across my mind. She straddled my thighs then crushed her mouth to mine. The slickness of her body when I entered. The tightness that followed. The way she would pant right in my ear as she pressed her tits into my face.

Then other memories came back to me.

Her eyes opened and looked into mine, tired and rested at the same time. "You stayed." Then this smile came on to her face, a smile so brilliant it was like the sun on a summer morning. Her hand reached for mine, stopping on my pec, right above my heart, like she wanted to feel it beat.

"You okay?" The voice shattered my daydream. Serenity was naked in front of me, on her knees as she worked my jeans.

Reality set in. It was dark. I was empty.

She was a beautiful woman, but I found myself utterly disappointed by everything about her. "No."

"What do you mean no?" she asked.

"No, I'm not okay." I got up from the couch and put my shirt back on. "Keep the money. I've got to go."

12

LAURA

Lucas and I just left. Catherine is alone.

Thanks, Victor. I headed to their apartment, knowing I'd have a couple hours alone with my sister before Lucas returned. Having Victor on my side made my life a lot easier. I wouldn't be able to pull off any of this without him.

The butler let me inside, and my sister didn't make any excuses not to see me.

When she caught sight of me, she immediately flocked to me. "Laura, are you okay?" Her eyes immediately went to my arm, where you could see the nasty scar I'd carry for the rest of my life.

"I'm fine." I looked at her arm, pleased to see it was no longer in a sling. "What about you?"

"A lot better than you." When she looked up, she saw me smiling. "What?"

"It's nice to see you care about me."

Her eyes dropped like she was embarrassed. "I was just worried after I heard what happened…" We moved into the drawing room, and her butler set out appetizers for us to enjoy without being told.

We were quiet for a while, like we didn't know what to say to each other.

"Daddy felt really bad afterward…"

Sure he did. "He apologized to me." *And I would never accept the apology.*

"I can't believe it came to that."

And it didn't have to come to that.

"You aren't with that guy anymore?"

That guy. He was so much more than *that guy.* "We broke up about a month ago."

"It was for the best."

If Lucas got hit by a semi, that would be for the best. "How are things with Lucas?"

"Good. Really good."

"Because he hasn't hit you in a month?" I asked sarcastically.

She directed her eyes elsewhere.

After escaping Bartholomew's wrath, my father's men were probably high on their win, so Lucas had other things to focus on besides tormenting my sister. When I took down my father, I was tempted to take Lucas too.

"I hear you and Victor are spending time together." My sister turned her gaze back on me, her eyes trying to pry into my mind.

Victor wouldn't voluntarily give up information, which meant Lucas had asked. If Victor started blabbing about it, it would come off as suspicious, because he had never been much of a talker, especially about his personal life. "It's nothing serious."

"You've had dinner together a few times."

"Are you guys spying on us?"

She quickly looked away.

So, I was being followed. Night and day.

"Victor is a good guy," she said. "I think he deserves another chance."

"You mean I deserve another chance?" I asked. "Because he's the one who divorced me." She was too young to really remember.

"I think true love always deserves a second chance."

Which was why she'd had her arm broken. And who knows how many black eyes she'd received.

"Victor is a better man than Lucas. And Dad has always really liked him."

Because he followed orders like a dog.

"You think…you guys will get back together?"

"I don't know, Catherine. I just got out of a relationship."

"Like a month ago," she said. "That's plenty of time."

That month had passed in the blink of an eye. It felt like just yesterday when I woke up in the hospital with him at my bedside. It felt like just yesterday when we were shacked up in the hotel room in Paris, our sweaty bodies stuck together like glue. When he'd told me he slept around, I didn't believe him…or I didn't want to believe him. But after our last conversation, I wondered if he'd moved on.

I didn't want to think about it.

"And he lied to you," she said. "He was using you the entire time. You don't owe him anything."

Even if that were true, my heart continued to weep.

"Victor is handsome, strong, wealthy, and Dad likes him—"

"You're really pushing for this, aren't you?"

"Well, it would be a dream come true. We could be a close family again. I know nothing would make Daddy happier."

Yes, having me under his thumb would really bring him joy.

"Victor said you two were really happy once."

It was so long ago it was hard to remember, but we had been happy. If I hadn't been raped, we'd probably still be married, about to celebrate our ninth wedding anniversary, having two little ones running around. "Catherine?"

"Yeah?"

"How would you feel if Victor were hurting me?"

All the color drained from her face.

"How would you feel if you knew he'd given me a broken arm?"

"That's not fair—"

"It is fair, Catherine. Maybe you don't care about yourself as much as you should, so imagining it happening to someone you love will help you understand. You don't have kids, so it would be easy for you to leave."

"Easy? I told you what would happen if I did that. I would lose everything."

"And money is more important than happiness?"

"Laura, money *is* happiness."

That was all my family cared about. Money and power. And if that were ever threatened, they would do anything to protect it. Literally. "Happiness is living a life that doesn't revolve around money. Happiness is being at peace with whatever hand you've been dealt. You're dependent on something for joy, which means you're a prisoner to it, which means you'll never truly be happy."

Victor sat across from me in the restaurant, wearing a tight shirt on his muscled arms. He'd shaved that morning, so his hard jawline was on display. I used to think he was the most handsome man I'd ever seen, but now he came in second to someone else.

"Not hungry?" Victor had his arms on the table, a fork in one hand and a knife in the other.

"Not so much."

"Didn't go well with Catherine?"

"She's brainwashed."

"I'll do all I can to keep Lucas on his best behavior."

"I appreciate that, but that's not your responsibility. Catherine should leave him."

"Catherine has never known anything outside her father's world. I'm not surprised."

"And he did that by design." He liked everything to be under his control. That included people.

He took a few bites of his food then washed it down with red wine.

"Catherine told me I'm being watched."

"I figured you would be."

"Are they watching you too?"

"I don't think so. Leonardo knows I'd been trying to make things right with you long before this all happened. I'm sure he assumes I'm pouncing because you're available again."

I looked down at my food, uncomfortable by what he'd said. "How's your mom?"

"The same. Still drops off meals on a weekly basis."

"That's ironic since I never cooked for you anyway."

He gave a shrug. "She's upset that I'm still a bachelor. Worries about me."

"And your dad?"

Now his eyes flinched. "Passed away a couple years ago."

My heart gave a tug because I'd loved his parents. They were good people. "I'm sorry, Victor."

"Years pass, and it gets better…but only so much."

"If it helps…I know how you feel."

His eyes locked on mine. "I know you do—and I wish you didn't."

Silence stretched between us. It went on for a long time, neither one of us knowing what to say.

Then he spoke again. "Your father is having this big party next weekend. I think you should come with me."

"Really?"

"You need to start spending time with him if you want this plan to work."

It was ironic. I wanted to earn his trust and affection, but I didn't actually want to spend time with him. "I guess."

"And it's a chance for them to see us together instead of spying on us."

"Yeah..."

"So that's a yes?"

"Guess it is."

I checked my appearance in the full-length mirror. A little black dress with my mother's diamond earrings.

Sky-high heels that hurt my feet the moment I put them on. A knock sounded on the door, and I felt a bit sick.

Sick for a lot of reasons.

When Victor saw me, his eyes quickly dragged over my body like he couldn't resist a look. He was in a suit, and he always looked handsome in a suit. He didn't say a word as we left the apartment and headed to his car downstairs.

The drive was spent in silence.

My phone was in my clutch. My stomach was in my throat.

We arrived at the party, the valet took the car, and we walked inside.

Victor's hand went to my lower back.

I almost jumped out of my skin when he touched me.

He caught my eye. "Is this okay?"

No one had touched me since Bartholomew. Even though it meant nothing, it felt like a betrayal. I gave a nod.

The party was at the Tuscan Rose, a hotel owned by old family friends. The ballroom was decorated with fresh flowers, and golden flutes hung from the ceiling. My father liked to show off his wealth with these elaborate parties he didn't even enjoy. He preferred to impress people he didn't like rather than having meaningful relationships with people he did like. I wasn't a psychologist, but I'd consider him a sociopath.

Victor got me a glass of champagne then returned his hand to the small of my back.

I felt like I was back in time, married to Victor, one of the daughters of the Skull King.

We got a lot of stares. My own family members studied me from across the room like a new type of mold that hadn't been discovered. They were nosy enough to stare, but not interested enough to actually speak to me.

"I don't miss this."

Victor drank from his champagne then looked at me. "I do, actually."

"You like these superficial parties?"

"No, but I like being with you."

The line caught me off guard. I didn't know what to say. Wasn't sure if I could meet his stare. "I feel like I'm pretty poor company."

"Why?"

"Well, I'm a very bitter and angry person…"

He gave a slight smile. "I guess I like angry and bitter." He took notice of the empty glass in my hand. "I'll get us another." He walked away, as if he wanted to give me a moment to recover from the unexpected affection he'd thrown at me.

I stood there alone, too stiff to mingle with people who didn't like me.

"You look beautiful, Laura."

I turned to see my father behind me. Anytime I was face-to-face with him, I wanted to strangle him. Bring him to his knees and make him sob for his life. The blood lust was so intense I nearly shattered the flute in my grasp. "Thank you, Leonardo."

His eyes showed their disappointment.

"Nice party."

"Thank you. Seems like everyone is having a good time."

Not everyone. "The short rib pockets are good. I've already eaten five."

"Haven't had a chance to try one."

"And the brie tarts. Those are good too."

He gave a smile. "You've always loved food."

Yep. The extra fifteen pounds I carried proved that. "I appreciate the finer things in life."

"Then you must get that from me."

I didn't get anything from you. "Maybe."

Victor returned and handed me the glass. The empty one was given to a passing waiter. "Beautiful party, sir," Victor said. "It's nice to have the night off."

"Well, you've earned it." My father gripped him by the shoulder, squeezed him like he was the son he never had. "You're a good man, Victor."

"Thank you, sir."

My father gave us a final look before he walked off. When he returned to a group of people, his arm moved around the waist of a woman younger than I was. My disgust for him grew.

"I think he's buying it," I said.

"I do too." He drank from his flute. "Your coldness has made it seem genuine."

It was nice not to be completely fake.

"I have an idea," he volunteered.

"Yeah?"

"You're not going to like it."

"Then why even suggest it?"

"Because it'll work."

"Alright, I'm all ears." I faced Victor and prepared to hear a complex plan.

He held my gaze. "We get engaged."

My heart did a flop.

"It's exactly what he would want. You would get closer to the family, and you would become loyal to me—and, therefore, him. He'd drop his guard even more, and then you could sink your teeth into him. Make him think he has his daughter back for good."

"I think it would be obvious if we got engaged so soon."

"We would wait a couple weeks. Let them see me sleep overnight at your apartment."

"If we do that, you're sleeping on the couch."

I caught a glance of disappointment he couldn't cover. "That's fine."

It was a good idea, even if I personally didn't like it. "Alright."

A couple nights later, we went out to dinner—then back to my place.

When my father watched me, he thought he saw the beginning of a rekindled relationship, but what he actually saw was two people planning to shoot him to death. It was nice to have the upper hand—even if he didn't know it.

I'd rented a small apartment that I'd found online. The owner was on vacation for the summer, so he rented out the place to someone for extra cash. That someone was me. It had one bedroom, a sitting room with a dining table, and a little kitchen. It was bigger than my apartment in Paris, so it was an upgrade, and it was a fraction of the price of my Parisian place.

Victor entered, took a quick look around, and gave a nod. "Nice place."

We used to live in a beautiful apartment, two entire floors, a formal dining room for entertaining. It was nothing compared to my father's estate, but it was still a dream home for most people. We'd sold the place and split the equity, and I bet Victor had moved in to another place even better than the last.

We both sat on the couch.

I wasn't sure how to entertain him now that dinner was over. It felt strange to be alone with him in the privacy of my home. If he were Bartholomew, we would already be naked and in bed, my face in the pillow and my ass proudly in the air.

I really needed to stop thinking about him.

I grabbed the remote and turned on the TV. "You want some wine?"

He nodded. "Sure."

I opened a bottle, and we drank as we watched TV, neither one of us talking. We did that for a couple hours before it was time for bed. I found an extra blanket and pillow in the closet and tossed it on the couch. "Good night."

Victor took off his shoes then stood up to pull his shirt over his head. Then he moved to his jeans.

"Whoa...what are you doing?"

He stilled and looked at me, his body hard and chiseled but not as ripped as Bartholomew's. "It's too hot, Laura." He continued his undressing, unbuttoning his jeans and pulling them off.

"Well...goodnight." I went into my bedroom, locked the door, and went to sleep.

13

BARTHOLOMEW

The bar was empty except for Benton and me.

He'd asked if I wanted to come over, but I didn't want anyone to see me visit his residence, not when my men were no longer trustworthy. A knife could dig into my back at any moment, and having eyes in the back of my head would only keep me alive for so long.

Benton must have said something I didn't hear because he said, "Bartholomew?"

I turned to look at him. "Yeah?"

"I just told you Constance had the baby."

"Oh…congratulations." I raised my glass to him then took a drink.

Benton studied me with his bright-blue eyes, the same eyes his brother had. "What's happened?"

"What's happened?" I asked as I watched my square ice cubes slide over the bottom. "My own men want me dead…and Laura is sleeping with her good-for-nothing ex. That's what's happened."

"How do you know this?"

"I have men tailing her."

"You think that's healthy?"

"I did it to keep her safe. Didn't expect her to shack up with that piece of shit."

"You don't know that for sure."

"He entered her apartment at ten in the evening and stayed until morning." I threw the glass at the wall and found some satisfaction in the way it shattered. "I think it's pretty clear."

The bartender immediately made me another.

How long until I broke this one too?

Good thing I owned the place.

"You're the one who ended things, Bartholomew."

"Not because I wanted to."

"It's been a month—"

"You see me fucking around?" I took a drink.

"But that's not what you told her."

"She didn't believe me."

"Maybe she believes you now."

I stared into my glass, watching the amber color swish around the translucent ice cubes.

"You shouldn't gamble if you can't afford to lose."

"Is this your way of trying to make me feel better?" I asked coldly. "Putting all the blame on me?"

"I'm giving it to you straight, Bartholomew. Like I always do."

I rested the glass against my temple, to cool the headache as well as the rage. "I'm so fucked, man."

"You need to kill Silas."

"If I do that, they'll all turn on me."

"Then you need to find a resolution."

"I'm pretty sure Silas doesn't want one. He's moving his pieces across the board, and I'm struggling to protect my queen."

"Then surround yourself with the ones you can trust."

I kept the glass there. "You know what's sad? I'm not sure who that is anymore." I stared at my hollow expression in the mirror on the wall, seeing the way my eyes were sunken, the way I'd aged a decade in just a month.

"You gave up everything for her—and you can't take her back?"

I set the glass down.

"Walk away from the Chasseurs. Get your woman. Be happy."

"There's no running from this. They'll hunt me down—and Laura is the last person I want with me when that happens." I tilted my head back and drank the rest in a single go. Scotch was a better painkiller than any kind of pill. "And I don't trust her."

"You gave her an impossible choice—"

"Doesn't matter."

"If it doesn't matter, why are you upset about her sleeping with someone else?" Benton asked. "You're sitting here drinking yourself to death over a woman."

I gently rotated the glass, making wet circles on the counter. "Because it was real...every moment...every night...all of it."

14

LAURA

My father had made a generous donation to the biggest Catholic church in Florence, and that somehow translated into an extravagant and unnecessary party. I rarely interacted with my father. It was always indirect, maybe a simple acknowledgment across the room, maybe a hand on the shoulder—but that was it.

I knew I needed to do more if I was going to execute this plan.

Victor returned to me, a glass of champagne in his hand.

Bartholomew wouldn't be caught dead drinking that. The man only drank the hard stuff and water—occasionally wine.

His hand went to my waist. "We've never shared a kiss in public."

I met his gaze, seeing the expectant look in his eyes. "I think sleeping over at my apartment is enough."

He didn't hide his disappointment. "I asked for your father's blessing."

My heart sank because this just became real. "What did he say?"

"He wouldn't give it to me."

My eyes narrowed in surprise. "What?"

"He said that you're a grown woman and don't need his blessing."

No patriarchal misogyny? No sexist bullshit? No twisted sense of ownership?

"But he hopes you say yes."

"That's the last thing I expected him to say."

"Me too." He finished his champagne then left the empty glass with a passing waiter. "Ready to get out of here?"

I was ready the moment I got here. "Sure."

We left the building across the street from the gorgeous church, the same one where we'd gotten married. Instead of calling the driver to pick us up, Victor took my hand, and we crossed the busy road to the entrance of the church.

"What are we doing?"

"I want to show you something." He pushed the door open, and despite the fact that it was after hours, it wasn't locked.

We entered the beautiful church made of medieval stone, surrounded by sculptures that had survived hundreds of years. When we walked down the aisle, I saw the sea of hundreds of candles, the white rose petals that were sprinkled everywhere.

Then he got down on one knee.

The last thing I expected.

He opened the box with the ring—the same ring he'd given to me a decade ago. "Love always deserves a second chance. Will you marry me—again?"

"Victor..." I didn't know what to say. We agreed the engagement would be a sham, but he made it feel as real as the first time he asked. "I said I would consider giving you a chance when I was ready, but this—"

He slipped the ring onto my finger without waiting for an answer and got to his feet. "And if you do, you'll know that I'm ready whenever you are."

A knock sounded on the door.

I was alone in my apartment, just finished lunch, and now I was painting my toenails on the couch. It wasn't Victor, because he always texted me before he stopped by. Another option popped into my head, but we hadn't spoken in weeks, and I knew it wasn't him.

I opened the door—and came face-to-face with *him*.

My father.

It caught me by surprise, and I couldn't keep a straight face as I looked into the eyes of my nemesis. I blurted the first thing that came to mind. "What—what are you doing here?"

"Can I come in?"

"Uh..." I hadn't expected company, let alone him. "Sure."

My father walked inside, scanned my tiny apartment with indifference, then helped himself to a chair at my dining table.

He probably thought I lived in utter ruin compared to him.

I took a seat across from him without offering water or wine. I was still shaken by his unexpected visit.

His hands came together on the table, and he gave me a faint smile.

I couldn't remember the last time I'd seen him smile. "So...what are you doing here?" I repeated.

"Victor told me the news." He glanced down to my left hand where my diamond ring was visible.

I'd just gone out to get lunch and had put it on before I left. Otherwise, I wouldn't be wearing it. I didn't wear a fake engagement ring for fun.

"I wanted to share my congratulations."

"Well...thanks."

"And I wanted to make sure this is what you really want."

My skin prickled.

"Victor told me Bartholomew hurt you pretty badly."

I couldn't believe I was having this conversation with my father. Even when we were on the best terms, it was still weird. "I don't want to talk about him." It hurt even to think of him. My mind wandered to other things, like who he had moved on to and if he'd forgotten about me altogether.

"I know Victor must feel like a safe option after that relationship."

"You think Victor is a rebound?"

"Your words. Not mine. But truth be told, I don't think Victor cares if that's what he is. He wants you in whatever capacity you will take him."

Was he here to make me feel guilty? "You don't think I'm good enough for him?"

"I just don't want you to feel rushed to settle down because of your broken heart."

I was only rushed to kill this motherfucker. "If that incident had never happened, I think Victor and I would have made it."

"I do too."

"And being with him again makes me realize what was taken from us."

He gave a nod.

"Love always deserves a second chance."

"It does." Now his eyes were focused on me, like his words implied a whole lot more. "It always does…"

I carried my bag of groceries up the stairs then fumbled with the key in the lock as I tried to balance one of the bags at the same time. I used my knee to stabilize everything, and then the bag tilted too far and toppled over. Oranges rolled across the floor. "Motherfucker." I finally got the door unlocked and pushed it ajar before I picked up the mess. A couple eggs cracked, but most of the stuff was unharmed.

I carried the bags into the kitchen and put everything away, except for the three cracked eggs that got yolk all over the paper bag. I had to throw it away instead of recycling it, and then I scrubbed my hands clean to get the salmonella off my skin.

I headed back into the living room—and jumped out of my skin.

The curtains over the main window were drawn closed, not by me, and in the shadow sat a man in one of the armchairs.

It took a moment for my vision to adjust. To recognize the angry coffee-colored eyes that burned my skin with the heat of volcanic lava. My heart raced so quickly that my lungs couldn't keep up with the demand, and I felt a little faint.

He'd skipped the leather jacket because it was too hot for anything but his black t-shirt. He was in dark jeans, and I could see his signature boots because one ankle was propped on the opposite knee. His elbow was on one of the armrests, his curled fingers underneath his chin.

I had no words.

Time passed and we stayed still, our eyes looking at each other in the dark.

I still couldn't find anything to say.

He got to his feet, and then his boots thudded against the hardwood as he came toward me, coming into the light from the kitchen behind me. Now his features were on full display—and I'd never seen him angrier. "Six weeks. That's all it took to forget me. *Six fucking weeks.*"

I'd been so surprised by his visit I didn't have time to ponder the reason he came.

"He's a coward, Laura. A goddamn coward."

I breathed hard, still unnerved by his ambush.

"You think the second time will be any different from the first? I wasn't safe enough for you, but this asshole is?"

It took time for me to gather my bearings, to stifle the scream in my heart. "You have a lot of nerve, Bartholomew."

He stepped closer to me, his dark eyebrows furrowed. "*I* have a lot of nerve?"

"You dumped me, remember? What do you care?"

"No, *you* dumped me," he snapped. "Let's not rewrite history. You only wanted me back when you realized you'd made the wrong choice. Don't paint me as the asshole. I don't settle for less than what I deserve—big difference. You, on the other hand, are selling yourself short if you think that man can make you happy. If you think he can make you come the way I do." He didn't yell, but he didn't speak calmly either. With every word, he suppressed his rage. The slight tremors in his body told me just how angry he was.

"Bartholomew, why are you here?"

His eyes narrowed.

"You don't want me, so why the fuck are you here?" Now I yelled. "I begged you for another chance. Apologized for my screwup I don't know how many times. The answer was no. Over and over. So why do you care if I want to marry Victor?"

He said nothing, but his eyes continued to burn with his fury. Every time I spoke, he seemed to get angrier, like every word out of my mouth was gasoline and his rage was the match.

"I may have broken things off between us, but you're the one who ended it for good."

"Not because I wanted to—"

"But you did—"

"Because I was angry. Angry that I'd sacrificed the world for a woman who wouldn't do the same for me. You hurt me—and I don't say those words lightly. I don't admit that kind of shit to anyone." He slammed his fist into his chest like a caveman. "But you fucking broke me."

Nothing he'd said hurt me as much as that. "You broke me too, Bartholomew."

"I never betrayed you—"

"But you broke me when you walked away."

"Really? Because it seems like you're doing just fine." He glanced down to the ring on my left hand, a ring I'd worn for two years. When he looked at me again, he was vicious once more.

I yanked it off my finger and set it on the dining table. "It doesn't mean anything."

His eyes narrowed.

"Victor and I are working together to bring down my father. It's just part of the plan."

His reaction remained stiff, like it took him longer than usual to understand the implications.

"We aren't seeing each other. We're just...friends, I guess."

It took a while for the anger to release its grip on his features. Slowly, the tremors stopped, the cords stopped popping out of his neck with the same prominence. He sheathed his rage, but a wisp of temper was still in his eyes.

"You can go now."

He second-guessed my words with his eyes.

"You don't want me, but you don't want anyone else to have me."

His arms hung at his sides, the prominent veins like rivers down his skin. He took a step closer to me as those brown eyes absorbed my soul. "I've always wanted you, sweetheart. That's never been the issue."

My breathing deepened, and I tried to cover it by crossing my arms over my chest.

He came closer to me. We were running out of space. Now he was so close I could smell him. Smell the sheets against my face first thing in the morning. Smell the smoke from his cigars, the vapors from his scotch. It sent a shiver down my spine.

He dipped his head, and I knew that kiss would bring me to my knees.

So I turned away. "I can't do this again..." I avoided his eyes as long as I could. It took time to find the strength to meet his stare.

His angry stare.

"If I hadn't warned my father, you would have killed him...and it would have ended anyway."

"You want him dead yourself."

"But I never would have known that."

He stared, his eyes intense with longing.

"I can't lose you again. It's been so hard..." Tears welled in my eyes, but I made sure they didn't fall. "There's no scenario where this can work between us. It just...doesn't make sense."

His hand slid into my hair all the way to the nape of my neck. Then he fisted it like reins to a horse and tugged my head back to look at him once more. His eyes commanded mine, bringing our souls together as well as our eyes. "Then we'll make it work this time."

His mouth closed over mine for the softest kiss he'd ever given me. It was an introduction between our lips, a break before the storm. He took my bottom lip and gave it a gentle bite before he turned his head and kissed me harder, his hand supporting the back of my head.

It took a moment for my body to come alive, to understand this was real and not just a fantasy as my fingers slid into my panties. My mouth responded as the fire reached me, and I appreciated the taste of his mouth, the way his beard scratched me as we turned our heads to kiss in a different position. It was the closest thing to time travel. I felt like I was back in the hotel room, him about to devour all of me and leaving nothing left.

My hands yanked his t-shirt over his head, and my fingers felt his warm skin. They remembered him perfectly, the trace of his body, the way his chest connected to his tight stomach. I explored all the muscles of his arms and shoulders, felt like an artist molding a sculpture of a Roman soldier.

My hands moved to his jeans next, anxious to get that dick inside me as quickly as possible.

He kicked off his boots as his jeans were tugged to his knees. His boxers came with them, and that enormous dick with all its distinctive grooves and veins came free. He didn't give me a chance to stare because he was ripping off my clothes with a lot more urgency than I'd just shown him.

Everything came off, my shoes kicked aside, my panties on the floor, my bra landing perfectly on the corner of one of the armchairs.

He got me on the bed, our weight making the old mattress dip. My thighs were already open and secured around his hips. My nails were hooked into his back, and I yanked him to me, desperate for his size to stretch me like old times.

But he hesitated.

He started to move away.

My ankles locked together and kept him in place. "I haven't slept with him."

His eyes locked on mine, his skin tinted red with arousal, his eyes dark with desire.

"And I know you haven't been with anyone either." I didn't believe a word of his lies. He'd just wanted to hurt me—and it didn't work.

He came back to me, guided himself inside, and then he sank.

"Oh god..." My nails sliced into his skin as I felt every inch of him buried inside me. "Bartholomew." I could feel him throb. He was harder than I ever remembered.

One of his arms hooked behind my knee and opened me farther. He shifted upward, his face above mine, and he rocked into me with even strokes, hitting me deep every time, his hot skin rubbing against my clit over and over.

I was already there. Ready to catch on fire. My nails dug into his ass, and I yanked him over and over, the match lit and the wood crackling. "Yes..." It was embarrassing how quick it was, but feeling his dick instead of my fingers made all the difference. Seeing his intense eyes claim me like that was always my undoing. I came so hard my moans turned into whimpers. The tears I'd restrained earlier came free as rivers down my cheeks. It was so good, making me sink my top teeth into his shoulder because my body wouldn't stay still. My hips bucked. My sex squeezed his with an iron grip.

How did I go six weeks without this?

My nails were deep in his back with my mouth against his ear. "I miss feeling you come inside me..."

A small earthquake moved through his body, a shiver I could feel under my fingertips. His thrusts became deeper, and he grabbed me by the neck and forced me back, my eyes on him. His thumb pressed against my bottom lip as his thrusts quickened, pounding into the finish line.

He came with a sexy moan, his hard face becoming even harder as he gave it all to me. "You want more, sweetheart?"

I brought his lips to mine and kissed him, feeling his hardness remain. "Please..."

I cooked dinner in the kitchen, for two instead of one, and then brought it to the dining table.

He sat there shirtless, in just his black boxers, his hair messy from my anxious fingers. The curtain was still drawn closed, so we couldn't enjoy the view of the city at night. He watched me serve him, his eyes on me instead of the food.

I sat across from him with my plate, wearing his t-shirt, like we were in my apartment in Paris. It was a mediocre dinner of grilled chicken with vegetables and rice, but I'd been trying to stick to a healthy diet instead of pasta and bread all the time.

He ate with his elbows on the table, disregarding all manners, being a typical man.

I looked at him.

He looked at me.

He'd been there since that afternoon, but it still felt like a dream.

A wet dream.

We shared a bottle of wine, and despite our time apart, we had nothing to say.

I was just happy to be with him. Deliriously happy.

He didn't compliment my cooking. He probably couldn't even taste it because I was still all over his tongue.

When the meal was over, we stared at each other.

I drank from my glass, admiring the view of the most gorgeous man I'd ever seen. Hard. Chiseled. Intense.

Mine.

I wondered if he was thinking the same thing.

"I'll tell Victor in the morning." I felt bad using him when I wouldn't be able to uphold my end of the deal. He would probably cancel the whole thing, but I'd find another way to accomplish my goals.

"Tell me everything that's happened with him." Now he was serious, the drug kingpin.

"As in, our plan?"

"Yes. From the beginning."

"Well, I spoke to my father first, told him how hurt I was. My father said he noticed the way Victor looked at me, and that gave me an idea. I asked if Victor wanted to help me destroy Leonardo, and he agreed. Not just because I asked, but because he was angry with the way my father treated me."

"But he made a condition."

"Yes. That I'd be willing to give him another chance... whenever I was ready to."

Bartholomew's stare was hard, back to his usual poker face. "And you meant that?"

"I guess." I was so desperate to achieve my goals, I would have sold my soul to the devil.

"You still have feelings for him." He spoke in a calm tone, like that assumption didn't infuriate him.

"Not the way I do for you."

His expression didn't change, like that wasn't enough for him.

"You've never been married, so it's hard to explain. I'll always care for him—and he'll always care for me. I guess there's this subtle attachment there, because of everything we shared. Maybe if there had been infidelity, we would have wound up hating each other, but that's not what happened."

Instead of releasing a tirade of insults, he stayed quiet. "And you trust him?"

"Trust him how?"

"Not to tell Leonardo all of this."

"I don't think he would do that…"

"I'm not so sure. He's worked for him his entire adult life. I doubt he would squander that for anything."

"What are you implying?" I asked.

He scratched the scruff of his jawline as he looked at the closed curtains, like he could see the city through the fabric. "You think the two of you are plotting against Leonardo, but I think the two of them are plotting against you."

"Victor wouldn't do that—"

"Not to hurt you." Bartholomew looked at me again. "Leonardo isn't stupid, and he knows what kind of daughter he has. He may brush off the incident like it wasn't a big deal, but he *knows* it's a big deal. He knows you're going to come for him. But he doesn't want to kill you. No man would want to kill his daughter unless he had no other choice." He shared his thoughts with me, laying out an analysis that hadn't even crossed my mind. "So he's trying to neutralize you. Tame your anger. Drop your hostility. Get his second daughter back into his life."

"It's certainly plausible. I don't put anything past my father. But there's no reason for Victor to do that."

Bartholomew stared. "None?"

My eyes flicked back and forth because I couldn't follow his insinuation.

"Perhaps a fake engagement will turn into a real one. Maybe false affection will become sincere. Maybe once you and your father make peace, you and Victor can pick up where you left off."

"You just…figured this out?"

"His request was suspicious. The only reason he should help you is because he's furious that his employer would shoot the woman he loves. The fact that he's trying to strike a deal with you in the midst of all that tells me there's more going on."

I hadn't thought of any of that.

"So Leonardo probably convinced him of this plan, and as an incentive, Victor would get back the life he lost. You two would live here in Florence. Get remarried. Maybe have a few kids. Victor would move up in the ranks. Maybe take Leonardo's place once the time came. It all makes sense."

"But you don't have any evidence."

"Unless I can eavesdrop on their conversations, I'll never have any evidence."

"I could ask Victor—"

"No." His arms crossed over his chest. "That's the worst thing you could do. And you can't tell him about me either."

"Why not?"

"Because if I'm in the picture again, he won't help you."

"I can't lead him on—"

"He's leading you on."

"We don't know that—"

"This is my world, sweetheart. I know how it works. I know how men like Leonardo think."

"I can't go on lying to Victor."

"He said he wanted a chance when you're ready. Then don't be ready."

"I did tell him I'm not over you."

"Then continue not to be over me."

I still felt guilty about the deceit. It was one thing to be open to the possibility, but knowing there was no chance whatsoever now made me feel like a big, fat liar. But if Bartholomew was right, there was no reason to feel guilty. I'd thought I was playing Leonardo, but Leonardo was playing me. "I really hope this isn't true…"

He stared at me with his dark eyes, enigmatic and commanding. "Trust me, sweetheart."

I hadn't trusted him last time—and that was my greatest mistake. "I do."

15

BARTHOLOMEW

Her head rested on my shoulder, her arm around my waist underneath the sheet. Her hair ran down my arm. One of her thighs rested on top of my leg. She smothered me with her smell, roses after a springtime rain.

My head turned, and I dragged my lips across her hairline before I gave her a kiss.

She squeezed me a little tighter in response.

It was dark outside, and the only light in the apartment was from the lamp on her nightstand. Our phones were on the surface, blank with inactivity. The world was quiet, and it was just the two of us wrapped in this bubble of tranquility.

Finally, I wasn't angry.

I wasn't happy either.

I'd found peace.

When Bleu had told me she was engaged to that coward, I'd boarded my jet without packing a bag and took off. It was an emotional impulse, an attack that would go nowhere, but I couldn't stop myself from airing my grievances, from telling Laura how much she'd ruined me.

I hadn't expected it to end like this.

She changed her position, propping herself on her elbow so she could look at me. "How long are you staying?"

"I should leave in the morning." I shouldn't have come in the first place. Had too much shit to do.

Her brilliant eyes flashed in disappointment. "When will you be back?"

"Not sure."

"I can come to Paris—"

"You can't leave. Not if you want to finish what you started." I thought she should abandon this vendetta, but I knew it was too important to her. Maybe they'd double-crossed her, but she could triple-cross them. "If you return to Paris, they'll know why."

"Well, I can't go long without you…" Her hand felt my chest, felt my stomach, felt me everywhere. She worshipped my body like I'd just given her a wad of cash that could buy her an apartment. But she wanted me for me—no other reason.

"I'll come back when I can."

"And I'll just walk into the apartment and find you sitting in the shadows?"

"Yes."

"What if Victor is with me?"

"I'll hide until he leaves. Or kill him. Depends on my mood."

"My father stopped by my apartment one day…"

Too bad that wasn't today. I could have taken the opportunity to stab him in the neck. "What did he want?"

"To talk to me about Victor." Her voice was quiet, as if she was reliving that intimate conversation. "How are things at work?"

If only she knew. "Busy."

"Have you reconsidered attacking my father?"

It might make things better with my men, but I would forfeit my honor and self-respect. "It seems like you already have it covered."

"It's gonna be a while before I get what I want."

"He's waiting for the moment when you let bygones be bygones. Once you do, that's your chance."

"I knew if I did it too fast, he wouldn't believe me."

"Well, you're engaged to Victor now..." I hated saying those words, even if they weren't true, even if she'd been committed to me this entire time. Once Laura killed Leonardo, I might not be able to resist the temptation to kill Victor too. "The sooner you finish it, the sooner you can come home."

"Yeah."

I wasn't sure how I was going to handle all this time apart, seeing her whenever I had the time for a quick flight, to sneak around Leonardo's men that still tailed her everywhere. I had to get into her apartment before she returned and wait however long it took for her to come back. I was a busy man, and I didn't have that kind of time.

"Being here with you now…makes me want to give up everything and come back." Her fingers traced the scruff on my jaw, dragging along the hair to feel the coarseness against her fingertips.

That was exactly what I wanted her to do, but I knew it wasn't safe. Silas wanted my head removed from my body. The last thing I wanted was for Laura to get in my way.

"I can't believe I used to live like this…surrounded by all the bullshit. My sister is so brainwashed that I don't think I can help her. She'll live a life as a battered woman…or be killed at some point."

She was making herself suffer even more, forced to spend time with the people she despised, all in the name of revenge. Her anger would fade, and at some point, she might question if the investment was worth the payoff. She'd left her job for this. Left her city for this. Would live apart from me for this.

We lay in silence together, her fingertips continuing to explore my body like she didn't remember every little detail, every little scar, every place she'd ever kissed me.

"So…what kind of relationship is this?" Her eyes stayed down, unable to look at me as she asked the question.

I waited for her to look at me, because I wouldn't continue this conversation without her undivided attention.

She finally lifted her gaze.

"I'm your man. You're my woman. That kind of relationship."

Her fingertips slid down my neck and over my collarbone. Her espresso-colored eyes dropped to my lips as her nails pressed lightly into my skin absent-mindedly. Seconds passed as she continued her stare, then her plump lips separated slightly, like she wanted to feel my tongue slide through the opening.

It was like one of my fantasies when I was alone in my bedroom. Like one of my daydreams that I envisioned when someone boring spoke to me. I imagined this woman all over me, but now it wasn't my imagination.

I rolled her onto her back and dove my lips to her tits. Plump. Warm. Firm. I inhaled her scent as I buried my face in the crevasse between them. I kissed her, tasted her, sucked on her nipples until she winced.

Her fingers dug into my wild hair, and she arched her back, pressing her tits harder into me. She offered herself on a platter and begged me to take her.

I pinned her thighs back with my arms, folded her underneath me until she was trapped with no escape, and entered a pussy so slick it made me growl. "Fuck." I sank until I was fully inside, seeing the way her lips parted as she inhaled a gasp. Her hands gripped my arms, her nails made possessive marks on my skin, and she held on as I fucked her like I hadn't already had the honor.

She was dressed and ready to go, wearing a pink sundress with wedge heels, a purse over her arm. She looked like a flower in full bloom in the garden, but her eyes showed storm clouds.

Because I was leaving.

Well, she was leaving, and then I would leave afterward.

I was dressed in the clothes I'd arrived in, my mouth clean because I'd used her toothbrush to brush my teeth when I woke up. Her broken heart was visible in her sad eyes, and it was hard to walk out the door knowing the mess I left behind.

"What are you doing for money?"

The question snapped her out of her sadness. "My savings."

I was surprised it got her this far. "I'll make a transfer to your account."

"I just told you I have money."

But not much of it. "Spend my money instead of yours."

"But that's not what I want from you."

"And what do you want from me?" I would wire the money the second I got into the car, so an argument was pointless, and I knew how much this woman loved to argue. I changed the subject instead.

She faltered momentarily, like she didn't have a concrete answer. "You…"

I stood in front of her, watching the desire burn in her eyes like a bonfire. "It's time, sweetheart."

"No…" She moved into me, her arms securing around my neck, her face coming close to mine. "I just got you back." Her hand moved to the collar of my shirt and fisted it, wrinkling the delicate cotton, and she tugged me into her for a kiss.

I crushed her in my arms, my hand on her ass underneath the dress. All my lonely nights were spent wanting her and hating her at the same time. Now my chest tightened with more than just desire, because I'd never wanted to leave her less. "I'll return the first chance I get."

"But you're the boss. Can't you just stay here? Stay here like you did last time?" She abandoned her pride and begged, and I'd never loved hearing a woman beg before. I usually found it whiny and annoying, but with Laura, it was a turn-on.

I was in hot water and couldn't afford unnecessary vacations. "I'll come back, sweetheart." I gave her a final kiss before I let her go. "Take this." I reached into my pocket and pulled out another phone.

She stared at it in my hand. "Why?"

"Because I'm sure they've tapped yours." I set it on the nearby dresser. "And don't bring it with you. Leave it here, in your nightstand or under the mattress." I moved to the door then gestured for her to leave. I'd wait fifteen minutes to make sure Leonardo's men had taken the bait. Then my guys would notify me when it was safe to move. It felt like Laura and I were having a clandestine affair, but our relationship had become too meaningful to enjoy the thrill of sneaking around and meeting in beautiful hotel rooms.

She looked at me with heartbroken eyes, like she was afraid this was the last time she would see me, like I'd decided to end this relationship again instead of giving it another chance. "Be careful." She cupped my face and kissed me before she walked out the door.

The second she was gone, I was enveloped by the shadows of the dark apartment, the cold after her warmth had left. I was back to being alone, and while I used to thrive in solitude, it felt hollow now.

Hollow without her.

16

LAURA

The scene was ridiculous.

Catherine and I went shopping, and Victor and Lucas tagged along. We ended up in the market for lunch, the four of us sitting together like it was the good ol' days. Lucas didn't speak to me, hardly looked at me, so the mutual hatred was still thriving.

Victor tried to carry my bags like he was my boyfriend, but I shut that shit down quick. He sat across from me at the table, and I studied his expressions as I tried to figure out if he was lying to me.

If he'd double-crossed me.

That answer wouldn't be obvious in his features or the sound of his voice. Unless I found the evidence in his phone or overheard a private conversation, I would never know with complete certainty.

Victor held my gaze. "Everything okay, Laura?" His question drew the attention of both Catherine and Lucas.

I'd had the best night of my life, carried invisible scars from his kisses and caresses, and then I had to say goodbye. No, I wasn't okay. I was heartbroken again, because I'd imagined if I had Bartholomew back in my life, he would stay. Now he was gone again, and I was stuck here, looking at the face of a man who may have betrayed me. "I have a headache." That was partially true, because I was going through withdrawal without my man.

"I can grab you something at the pharmacy," Victor offered.

"No, it's fine. I have something in my purse. Just took it a couple minutes ago."

Victor continued to stare at me across the table, ignoring his half-eaten pizza in front of him.

"Where should we go now?" Catherine asked. "Valentina?"

I couldn't afford the cheapest thing in that store, not even a belt. "Sure." Most of the day had been spent watching Catherine blow ridiculous amounts of father's money on shit she didn't even need while the three of us followed behind. I'd grabbed a couple things, but they were all from vendors on the street.

As we got up from the table, my phone vibrated with a notification.

My bank had received a wire transfer for a hundred thousand euros.

"Jesus..."

"What is it?" Victor asked.

I quickly deleted the notification so it would disappear from my phone. "Just saw a news headline." I returned my phone to my purse, and we left the market and returned to the street.

Victor continued to study me like he didn't believe me, but he didn't press me on it.

A couple days later, Victor and I had dinner together at my favorite restaurant. He always let me pick, and he always insisted on paying, even though Bartholomew had just dropped a small fortune into my bank account. I could leave my apartment and move in to the Four Seasons. I didn't want his money, but I couldn't deny it was a godsend. My savings had taken a serious hit, and very soon, I was going to run out of money. I'd pushed it to the back of my mind because my revenge was more important than whatever I had left, but he'd now fixed that problem for me.

I would spend it because I didn't have a choice, and if he hadn't given me that money, I would have had to ask Victor…and that would make me feel dirty.

We didn't say much over dinner. We spent a lot of time together now, so there wasn't always much to talk about. His eyes were on me most of the time, catching glimpses of my face when he thought I wasn't looking. "I feel like there's something wrong."

Guess I wasn't as good of an actress as I thought. "I guess I'm just confused…"

"About?"

"I don't know…it's complicated." I was making all of this up on the fly.

He moved closer to the table, resting his elbows on the tablecloth because the waiter had removed our dirty dishes. "Talk to me, Laura."

"I left my job. Left my apartment. Left everything to come here and kill my father. But now…I don't know."

"You're getting cold feet."

"I wouldn't call it cold feet. I just…feel differently. It's nice to spend time with my sister. It's nice to be home again. It's nice to…have a relationship with you. Maybe I'm just going crazy, but I'm not sure if I even want to hurt my father anymore…"

He didn't blink, hung on every word.

"I mean, I'm angry. A part of me will always be angry. But…I don't know… I'm not making any sense."

"Actually, it makes sense to me," he said. "Before everything happened, we were happy. You were happy. Now, it's like you're back in time. Why destroy something that makes you happy? Because if you did kill your father, it would destroy everything else. There'd be nothing left."

My heart sank because I saw it—the truth.

Bartholomew was right.

Victor had played me—and he'd played me good.

I made sure my expression didn't change as the truth sank in. My father knew everything. My father knew I was biding my time for the opportunity to torture him the way he'd tortured me. When he came to my apartment, he knew. When he made that comment about Victor...he was playing me.

I was such an idiot. "What about you? How do you feel?"

"How do I feel about what?"

"You said you wanted to hurt my father for what he did to me." The fact that that was a lie hurt even more, because he hadn't changed at all. He'd never stand up for me. He'd never defend me. He'd never be the man Bartholomew was.

"It was an asshole thing to do, and I'll always be upset about it. But there was no long-term damage to your arm. You made a full recovery, and you're right about what you said—that our lives would be forever different if he were dead."

No long-term damage? How about trauma? Heartbreak? Insatiable blood lust?

"I support whatever you decide."

Sure. "I'm not sure if my relationship with my father will ever be what it used to be. I was still loyal to him in our estrangement, but I'm not sure if I can ever be that loyal again. Just because I don't want him dead doesn't mean I trust him."

"That's fair."

"I'm just confused right now…"

"There's no rush. I've enjoyed the time we've spent together."

It took all my strength to say the words back and mean them. "Yeah…me too."

The second phone rang, and I quickly answered it. "Hey."

His deep voice was on the other line. "Hey, sweetheart."

We hadn't spoken in a couple days, and the second I heard his voice, I melted into a puddle. "I miss you…" I'd turned into one of those clingy women who couldn't give their man space. But there was so much I couldn't say during those six weeks apart, so I didn't hesitate to say it now. It still felt like a dream, having this man walk back into my life and look at me the way he used to.

A long stretch of silence passed, a buildup of tension.

"Are you still there?"

"Yes. Just enjoying your words."

"I missed you every day..."

"I missed you every night." My eyes closed, memorizing the sound of his voice, the way it wrapped around me like he was there with me. "How was your day?"

"It hasn't started."

"Oh, that's right. You just woke up."

"How was yours?"

"Eh."

"Eh?" he asked, slightly amused.

"I talked to Victor today. Told him I'm getting cold feet about killing my father."

He turned quiet.

"You were right... He's playing me."

"Did he say that?"

"No, but I could tell. The second I expressed my doubt, he encouraged me to drop the vendetta. It's exactly what he wants. For my father and me to get along, for me to take him back, for us to have the life we had seven years ago."

"I almost feel bad for him. *Almost*."

I didn't feel bad for him at all. He lied to me, so I didn't feel any remorse for leading him on. Why did he want a woman he had to manipulate to get in the first place? It didn't make any sense. "He should be angry for what my father did, but he doesn't care…he's never cared."

"You sound disappointed."

"I'm disappointed in myself for thinking I could trust him."

"In his defense, he's taking the path of least resistance. There's a very good chance you would end up dead if you really did try to kill your father, so this will keep you alive. It's better to settle for a good life than strive for a great one."

"You don't settle."

He was quiet for a while. "Because I'm a leader—not a follower like he is." I heard the sound of the lighter then the breath he took. He must have lit a cigar with his coffee, like people enjoyed a biscotti with their morning kick of caffeine.

I missed the smell of his cigars.

"What's your plan now?"

"I don't have a plan—not anymore." Not after I'd realized my enemies knew exactly what I was doing. "All I can do is lie and pretend I have a change of heart... And then when the opportunity presents itself...go for it. It's not exactly what I pictured, but I'll still catch him off guard."

"True."

"And then I can come home to you."

He stayed quiet. The silence continued on like he had no intention of saying anything. He just smoked his cigar and drank his coffee.

"Thank you for the money." When I checked my account today, I discovered I had even less than I realized. The cost of the apartment and food really added up. "I feel bad for taking it, but—"

"I'm your man, sweetheart. It's my job to take care of you."

I didn't even like it when a guy paid for dinner on a first date. I didn't accept handouts. I didn't accept loans. But I took Bartholomew's money, not because he was rich, but because it felt different. "How are things with you?"

"Same shit as always." He was never specific about his work.

"You can share your life with me, Bartholomew. You aren't going to scare me off." His livelihood wasn't important anymore. I'd become so attached that the risks his career imposed weren't nearly as dangerous as not having him. My broken heart hurt a lot more than that bullet.

"I had to blackmail the prime minister to keep our northern borders open, but the Prime Minister of Belgium is growing increasingly frustrated by the drugs that have suddenly flooded their streets. I'm afraid my threat to expose his affair and illegitimate heir won't be enough to keep business running, not when the crime is so apparent. But I have more product than I can sell before it expires. Without the Italian territory I'd intended to have as mine by now, I need another outlet. And if I don't succeed, my distributors will grow angry because they'll lose the money they invested. My men don't show the same allegiance to me they once did, so it's much harder to get shit done. Some still respect me, but some will never respect me again. Instead of actually doing my job, I spend my time trying to figure out how to do my job the way I once did. Croatia is still a strong territory, but it's so much smaller than France that it's not a substantial addition. Italy is a comparable country, and it's the gateway to other desirable places, like Greece and the Middle East."

I listened to all of this in both reverence and fear. He sounded like a suit on Wall Street talking about stocks and bonds, but instead of legal investments, it was drugs. I had no response, not when I couldn't grasp the depth of his work. "I'm sorry I made such a mess for you."

"It wasn't a dig, sweetheart."

"I know, but I'm still sorry."

It turned quiet.

I spoke again. "Do you ever think about leaving?"

"Leaving what?"

"Your work."

"To do what?"

"I don't know..." *Have a quiet life with me, maybe.*

"No, I never think about it."

Another wave of silence ensued. It kept going, lasting for so long it seemed like he wasn't there anymore.

He eventually spoke again. "I have to go."

"Alright."

"Goodnight, sweetheart."

"Good morning, vampire..."

My father hosted dinner at his estate, in the same courtyard where we'd celebrated Uncle Tony's life. It was small, only ten of us, Victor and Lucas, along with some of the other men he considered family.

The sun didn't set until nine these days, so we still had sunlight as we sat near the fountain, the Tuscan warmth making us sweat on the back of our necks. I took the seat beside Victor, staying as far away from my father as possible. Victor's deception made me loathe him even more.

I was still an outsider to most of them. His men hardly looked at me, and they certainly didn't talk to me.

Catherine was the life of the party, stealing all the attention because she was young, cute, and energetic. I could tell Lucas was annoyed by it, but he couldn't exactly slap her right in front of my father.

Not that he would do anything.

Victor drank from his wine then placed his hand on my thigh underneath the table. His movements were smooth and careless, like it was natural and not premeditated. His fingers rested just above my knee, right on my bare skin, and the touch made me feel so guilty, it was as if I'd slept with him.

Instinctively, I brushed his hand away, feeling like I was betraying Bartholomew for allowing it to happen.

Victor didn't try again, but he looked at me like I was in the wrong.

If Bartholomew were there…everyone except my sister and I would be dead right now.

I ignored Victor's gaze and took a drink of my wine.

My father gave a loud laugh when Lucas said something funny, oblivious to the intensity between Victor and me.

I didn't even know Lucas could be funny because he was too busy being an asshole.

"Excuse us." Victor rose from the table then pulled back my chair, forcing me to step away from the table.

We entered the house and walked away from the windows.

When he rounded on me, he looked furious. "You said you would give me a chance, but you can't bear my touch." Flames burned in his eyes like I'd just thrown gasoline on top. "How is that giving me a chance?"

Wow, he had the audacity to be mad at me? "I said I would give you a chance when I was ready—"

"It's been two months. That's plenty of time—"

"That's nothing when you're in love."

His entire body flinched like my words were blasphemy. His eyes shifted back and forth between mine, physically disturbed by the confession.

My feelings had been locked up tight for so long that I'd never admitted it to myself, let alone another person, and Victor, of all people. But the feeling of love was as strong as the feeling of disgust when he touched me, just for two different men.

"You lied to me."

"No," I said. "I didn't. I said when I was ready—"

"You've been together this whole time—and you lied about it."

"What...?"

"Where did the hundred thousand come from?"

They watched my bank accounts? Or did they have access to all the notifications on my phone? Was Victor looking through it every time we were in the same room? "My financial well-being is none of your business."

"There's only one person who would send you that kind of money."

"Even if he did—"

"You lied to me." Now he raised his voice. "I never had a chance. Not a real one."

"You know what?" I snapped. "You're right. You never had a real chance, but it's not because of him. It's because *you're* the fucking liar. You told my father everything. You've been partners in this since the beginning."

His eyes turned guarded, but he didn't deny it.

"So, no, this was never going to work, Victor." I started to storm off.

He grabbed me by the wrist. "Laura."

"Let go of me."

His grip tightened. "Listen to me—"

"I don't trust a goddamn word out of your mouth."

"I meant every word I said to you. I was furious at what happened, but there's no scenario where you get what you want, Laura. I thought if we tempered your anger, we could be a family again. We could be what we used to be—"

"Fuck you." I twisted out of his grasp and marched off.

This time, he didn't follow me.

I stormed out of the house, heels tapping against the tile, heading to the entryway to retrieve my purse from the butler so I could leave that place. There was no point in staying in Florence now, not when the plan had blown up in my face.

"Laura."

Right after I grabbed my purse, he appeared, the patriarch. "You don't see it."

"See what?" I stayed several feet away like he had a knife.

"How much I care about you."

"Of course I don't—because you don't care about anyone but yourself."

He stepped closer to me.

Out of defiance, I stood my ground. All I had in my purse was some mace. I hadn't expected tonight to go down like this.

"I don't want to hurt you, Laura. And I certainly don't want to kill you." He didn't directly say it, but the threat was implied. "I thought we could be a family again. I thought we could put the past behind us and move forward."

"Never." The venom was heavy in my voice. I felt vulnerable, alone in his house, Bartholomew out of my reach.

A standoff ensued. My father stared at me with guarded eyes.

I did the same.

"Then heed my warning." His voice changed, speaking to me like a man who crossed him rather than his own daughter. "I will kill you—if you make me. So I suggest you leave, and I suggest you make sure our paths never cross again."

I knew he was capable of it, but hearing him say those words was another bullet in my flesh. My own father... freely admitting he could put me six feet under. It made me want to cry, but I didn't dare let the moisture grow behind my eyes. "You'll get what you deserve," I said, my voice now a whisper. "Someday."

17

BARTHOLOMEW

I lifted the bar off the floor and did my set, curling my biceps with the most weight I'd ever done. My day always started with a gym session, but I was pushing myself harder than I had before, needing an outlet to release my frustration.

I dropped the bar then my phone vibrated in my pocket. I pulled it out, glanced at the screen and saw Bleu's name, and then turned off my music so I could take the call. "Yes?"

"Laura landed in Paris an hour ago. She's back at her apartment."

I wore a blank stare, unsure what had transpired to make that happen. Maybe she missed me, but she wouldn't sacrifice all her hard work for a quick booty call. Something must have happened—something bad. "Thanks for letting me know."

"Sir?"

Great, there was more.

"The prime minister wishes to speak with you."

Tensions were escalating. The heat on his back had started to burn through his clothes. "He'll have to wait."

I let myself inside her apartment without knocking, seeing that she wasn't in the common areas. "Laura?"

She came out of the bedroom, barefoot in a sundress. It had thin little straps and barely contained her sexy breasts. She must have distracted everyone at the airport while she sat there and waited for her flight. "He figured it out." She was clearly shaken up because her hands weren't all over me like they usually were. "The money... he knew you were the only one who would have given it to me."

"How did they know about it?"

"I don't know."

It took me a second to figure it out. "You shouldn't have bank notifications on your phone like that. If someone steals your phone, they know more about you than they should."

"Well, I've been broke all my adult life, so I've never had anything to hide." She walked off, reaching for a bottle of wine in her cabinet, along with two glasses. She uncorked it and poured the red wine. When she took a drink, her lipstick smeared around the glass, and all I could think about was having that color around the base of my dick. "Fuck."

I approached the small kitchen island and took the other full glass without taking a drink.

She gripped the edge of the counter, her eyes not on me but somewhere else altogether.

I didn't interrogate her because I knew the information would flow naturally. Just had to give her time.

"He said he would kill me if he ever saw me again." She didn't look at me as she said it, like she was too embarrassed to admit the truth, not just to me, but herself. "My own father..." A sarcastic laugh escaped her lips, short and brief, bitter.

This was the moment people said they were sorry, but it didn't feel right to say that now. It was hollow and pointless.

"I would have killed him right then and there, but I didn't have the means."

I wanted to break my word and do the dirty work for her. Break his skull in her name. But if I didn't break my word for my men, I couldn't do it for her. I was in hot water as it was. Already looking over my shoulder every time I turned a corner.

"And Victor…he hasn't changed one bit."

Her wine was cheap and barely tolerable, but I drank it anyway. I preferred hard liquor, but I respected fine wine, the kind stored in cellars for decades, the kind picked from the best harvests in France and Italy.

She took another drink, finishing the glass. "I guess it's over…" Her eyes finally lifted to mine.

"I wish I could fix this for you."

Her eyes softened. "I know you do." She came around the kitchen island and slid her hands up my arms, snuggling into my body, her perky tits right against my chest. Her arms circled my neck, and she rested her forehead against my chin. The smell of springtime washed over me, coming from her skin and her hair. "But I'm happy to be home with you."

My arm circled her waist, while the other slid underneath her dress, over that fine ass and to the bare skin of her lower back. I enveloped her against me, keeping her close as I closed my eyes, feeling all the pain in my heart stop for a moment in time. I was the kind of man to hold a grudge—and hold it forever. But I wasn't angry with her anymore. All that resentment and rage had been replaced by a calming sense of peace.

She pulled her head back and tilted her chin to look at me, her lips slightly parted and her eyes eager. A tint was already in her cheeks from the wine, and her partially painted lips practically begged me to kiss her. I must have taken too long admiring the view, because she cupped my cheek and rose as high as she could on her tiptoes so she could kiss me.

My hand squeezed her ass as I pulled her into me. Her kiss was soft and gentle, but I took over and made it rough and hard. Our tongues danced together. Our breaths grew short. My hand continued to squeeze both cheeks under her dress.

No woman had ever made me harder.

My fingers grabbed her little thong and yanked it down to her thighs before I lifted her onto the kitchen counter. The glasses rolled off and shattered on the other side of the kitchen island. The bottle tipped over, and wine dumped onto the floor with a loud splatter.

Neither one of us noticed.

With her dress hiked to her waist, I tugged down my bottoms before I pulled her close.

I pushed inside, making myself right at home.

She gave a loud moan as she held on to me, her head rolled back, her hair everywhere. She lay back across the counter, and I pushed the dress higher, revealing the bottom swell of her sexy tits. I yanked it a little higher until I could see the sharp nipples.

With my hands on her hips, I fucked her on the kitchen counter, hard all the way through, never letting up. I made her mine all over again, pounded into her so hard her tits shook.

When she said my name, it started as a whisper, but by the time I made her come, it was a scream.

The romp in the kitchen wasn't enough.

We made it into the bedroom, and now she did all the fucking. Her palms were planted against my chest as she rocked her hips, rolling them forward and back, taking my dick with expert precision every time. Now her dress was off, so those tits were right in my face, covered with a layer of sweat that smelled like roses.

I was propped against the headboard, my hands on her hips, enjoying the sheath of her pussy over and over. It was like old times, our clandestine meetings in a dark hotel room, fucking like it was the first time we'd sunk our teeth into each other.

Her movements became inconsistent. So did her breaths, which turned shallow and short. Her eyes grew heavy, and her pants turned into incoherent moans—and then cries. The shimmer in her eyes was like dew on a winter morning. It shone in the early light and twinkled like Christmas lights. Then her hips bucked uncontrollably as she screamed. Her nails sharpened and dug deep into my flesh like little daggers. Her body gripped mine with the strength of a viper, squeezing harder and harder.

I'd waited long enough, so I enjoyed my high just as she finished hers. It'd been nearly a decade since I'd filled a woman, and it was addictive to have that luxury again.

Nothing made me feel more like a man than fucking Laura like this, her ass right on my balls, her skin against mine, our come mixed together.

She got off me then lay beside me, naked on top of the sheets, her beautiful skin glistening from her effort. Propped on one elbow as she was, the curves of her body were on display, and despite the fact that my dick had gone to rest, I was still turned on by the way she looked. When I'd looked at that naked hooker in the hotel room, I'd been so unaroused I'd felt like I was staring at another man.

I reached for my pants at the bedside and pulled out the cigar and lighter. I lit up without asking for permission because she'd granted it a long time ago. Against the headboard I smoked, and she lay there quietly, the two of us enjoying the comfortable silence.

She eventually grew cold and pulled the sheets over her perfect body.

I wanted to stay, but the streets called for my attention. "What will you do for work?"

"I'll go back to the office tomorrow. I told my clients I had a family emergency…which was somewhat true."

"You don't have to work if you don't want to."

"I like my job. I get to dress rich people in designer clothes and make them look amazing."

"If they're rich, you should charge more."

"I don't do it for the money."

"You should. Imagine the apartment you would have. Imagine the clothes you would wear."

She lifted her chin to look at me. "What's wrong with my apartment?"

I held her stare.

"Never pegged you as the snobby type…" There was a slight smile on her lips, like she wasn't truly offended by what I'd said.

"I'm not snobby. I just expect more out of life—as should you."

"Or you can learn to be happy with what you have."

"Only small-minded people feel that way—and you aren't small-minded." I continued to smoke my cigar, holding it between my fingers as my arm rested on my knee.

"Your ambition is sexy, but not all people think the same way."

I stared at her profile as I treasured what we had. I could be completely honest with her and she didn't call me an asshole. "If I bought you an apartment, would you accept it?"

"Wow, I didn't realize how much you hated this place."

"I just want you to have everything you deserve."

She didn't say anything for a while. "I appreciate the offer, but I like my apartment. I'd reconsider if the new apartment included you..." She didn't hold my gaze as she made the suggestion.

"You want to live with me?" It was hard to imagine at first, sharing my space with someone else, day and night, opening my closet and seeing dresses and heels on one side of it. When I walked into the bathroom, there would be perfume and makeup on the counter, a pink razor in the shower. The top drawer of my dresser would have her delicates, her brightly colored thongs and lacy bras. It would be an infringement on my space, my identity. But if she lived there...I'd see her wear my t-shirt to bed, see her strut across the room in just her panties when she got out of the shower, see her without makeup first thing in the morning.

She still didn't look at me. "Yes...if you asked."

I almost did.

But it would be wrong to ask, not when my own men wanted me dead. My residence was a possible location for a hit, and the last thing I wanted was Laura there, especially in the event that I wasn't.

So I said nothing.

It was awkward at first, as if she expected me to ask, and when I didn't, the tension slowly faded. "I have to go." I left the bed, put out the remainder of the cigar, and dressed in the clothes I'd arrived in.

She pulled on one of her oversized shirts. The material was thin, so her nipples were hard through the fabric. When she walked me to the door, she didn't seem angry or disappointed by my rejection. She still seemed happy that she had me at all.

When she looked at me like that, like I was the best thing that had ever happened to her, it did some crazy shit to me. Made me consider options I'd never considered before. Made me think of a different way of life.

She walked me to the door. "Good morning." She gave me a quick kiss goodbye.

"Goodnight, sweetheart."

18

LAURA

It'd been a long time since I'd been in my office. There were actually a couple cobwebs underneath the desk. I sent out some emails, made some calls, told my clients I was back in business—and would remain that way for the foreseeable future.

It was good to be back to work, back in Paris, back in my apartment, back with Bartholomew. But I still felt a bit empty after my father had threatened to kill me. I didn't expect much from him, but it was still hard to brush off his cruelty.

I wished I'd killed him.

But now I would never get that chance again.

The downside to having a vampire for a boyfriend was the opposite schedules. When I was at work, he was asleep. When I was asleep, he was at work. It was never an ideal time to text or call.

His message popped up on my screen. *You have plans tonight.*

I do? I hope they involve me getting laid…

If you play your cards right.

Looks like I'm wearing something slutty. Where are we going?

Dinner.

Wow, Bartholomew was taking me to dinner. That was a first.

I'll pick you up at 7.

I stuck with a little black dress, made of spandex so it was skintight, with two little straps over my shoulders. I paired it with gold jewelry and black heels. It was the first time I'd gone out in public with Bartholomew in Paris, and it made me nervous—like it was a first date.

It was definitely the first of its kind.

When he picked me up, I was surprised to see him in clothes other than his black jeans and boots.

The man actually owned a collared shirt.

And he looked *gooooood*.

I looked him up and down, so absorbed in my stare I missed the sight of him checking me out. "So, you do own other clothes."

He ignored what I said and fisted my hair as he kissed me. As always, his big hand squeezed my ass, sliding underneath the material to touch the flesh with his bare fingers. He always manhandled me when he saw me, but I didn't mind it in the least.

He pulled down one of the straps then yanked the dress so one of my tits popped out. He did that as he backed me into the wall.

"What about dinner?" I asked as he groped me against the wall, hiking up my dress and yanking down my thong. I was breathless, feeling his scorching kiss on my exposed neck.

"You think I'm not going to fuck you when you're dressed like that?" He turned me around and pushed me against the wall. He shoved himself inside me an instant later, his big dick hitting me deep.

I cried out because it hurt—but felt amazing.

He fucked me up against the wall, his flattened palm holding my stomach, his lips breathing at my ear. "Then I'll fuck you again when we get home."

I had to fix my makeup and comb my hair before we left because I looked like a goddamn train wreck. But it was worth it to get fucked like his whore. Now we sat together at the table, in one of the nicest restaurants, the kind that had a yearlong waitlist. I'd been there once because a billionaire client had taken me.

Bartholomew was so out of place for a restaurant like this, but he also fit perfectly. He knew how to order wine, knew how to conduct himself like he'd done this a hundred times. He seemed to have a secret life.

"Have you eaten here before?" I asked.

"Yes."

"Like, a lot?"

"Many times."

"You don't seem like a man who enjoys this sort of thing."

He grabbed the stem of his glass and took a drink. "Part of the job."

"Fine dining?" I asked. "You booked this reservation in advance but didn't want to waste it?"

"I didn't have a reservation."

"Then how did you get in?"

"I own it."

I stiffened at his announcement because that explanation made perfect sense and I should have guessed. He told me he owned a lot of businesses in Paris because it was the only way to wash all his money.

He grabbed the bottle and refilled my glass.

Sometimes I forgot who Bartholomew was. To me, he was just my lover, but to everyone else, he was a billionaire drug kingpin.

"Have you been here before?"

"Once—and I loved it."

"With whom?"

"A client." I noticed the way he ignored my compliment. Probably didn't care if people liked the restaurant or not. "He's super rich, so he was able to get a reservation." They asked for a fifty percent deposit, and that was five hundred euros. I didn't have that kind of money.

He drank from his glass again.

"This is our first time out… It's nice."

"I'm glad you're enjoying it."

"You don't do this sort of thing, do you?" I could tell this experience wasn't as fulfilling for him as it was for me.

"For business. Not pleasure."

"You've never taken a woman on a date before?"

He gave a subtle shake of his head. "Dinner just postpones sex, and sex is all I'm interested in."

"What about with me?"

His dark eyes were settled on me, still like a calm lake, a deep brown like the soil after a rain. The restaurant was decorated with gold and soft lighting, and it deepened the shadows under his jawline. Time seemed to pass differently for him than it did for everyone else, because long pauses of silence didn't unnerve him. "The situations aren't comparable."

"Why not?" I already knew the answer, but I wanted to hear him say it, to treasure the fact that we were together again, that he was mine and not someone else's. Our time together still felt like a dream after the nightmare of his absence.

"Because you're my woman."

The second the door was closed, he was on me.

The top of my dress was pulled down to expose my tits, and the bottom was hiked up to my stomach. He slid his thumbs inside my little black thong and pulled it over my ass before he guided me onto the bed.

The dress was a band around my stomach, and my heels were still secured to my ankles. I lay there and watched him get undressed, taking his time popping every button, his eyes glued to me. He pulled off the collared shirt, showing a ripped physique that was so strong and tight. His pants came next, that fat dick coming free and just as ready to fuck me as it had been before we'd left for the restaurant.

Fuck, he was so hot.

He moved up my body then positioned me the way he wanted, folding my legs like a pretzel, tilting my pelvis so he could slide right into my slickness.

"Wait."

He stilled, his eyes checking mine for unease.

My fingers slid into his hair, and I kissed him. A slow kiss, an embrace that was purposeful. I felt his lips. Felt his tongue. Took my time to treasure this man for the god he was.

He let me decide the pace, allowed me to slow down the heat until it was a gentle simmer. He grabbed my ankle, slipped off the heel, and planted my foot against his chest. I'd always been flexible, and that came in handy now as he molded me into what he wanted. With his lips on mine, he guided himself to my entrance and pressed hard against it like a firm kiss, and then sank past my flesh and dived into the wetness.

I breathed against his mouth as I felt him slide all the way in. My fingers were still in his thick hair as I confessed the depth of my feelings. "I love you." I said it against his lips, said it as I grabbed him as tightly as I could.

His lips pulled back, and he locked his gaze with mine. He started to rock, his stare hot and intense, claiming me with his mind like his body wasn't enough. He didn't fuck me the way he had earlier. He kept it slow because that was what I wanted, to take our time and really feel each other, to feel his heartbeat with mine.

He never said the words back. He vowed he would never tell me he loved me. Would never ask me to marry him. He seemed to keep that promise by maintaining his silence. He didn't reciprocate my feelings, but that didn't bother me because he didn't turn cold, didn't push me away. He stayed in the moment with me, desiring me just as much as he did before. He still made love to me as if he felt the same way—even if he didn't.

19

BARTHOLOMEW

I smoked the cigar and stared out the window.

The prime minister was at my mercy, and I continued to grind him until he had nothing left to give. But that expiration date would arrive soon, and the new frontier I'd acquired would close permanently.

I'd slept like shit last night, so I was awake in the middle of the day, looking at the tourists crawling all over the sidewalks like the goddamn plague. The rich always retreated to their summer homes in Lake Como to get away from all the bullshit. I stayed because I didn't have the luxury of working from my computer.

Bleu entered the parlor and took a seat at my side.

I gestured to the box of cigars, offering him one.

He didn't take it. "It's happening tonight."

I took a deep drag before I released the heavy cloud of smoke. "How many guys?"

"I don't know."

"Where?"

"I don't know that either. I heard from Nico, who heard from Tyler, who heard from Cameron. This information isn't solid, but we should take it seriously. He must intend to get you alone—or he's paid off your guys."

If that were true, Bleu was the only man I could trust. "I'll be at the bar tonight—make sure the right people know."

"What's your plan?"

"To deal with him—one-on-one."

I sat at the bar alone, in my t-shirt and jeans, sitting on the stool with a cool glass in my hand. There were a few other people there, people who should leave soon because they would probably end up shot if they didn't.

I kept my back to the window, knowing it was bulletproof because I owned the place.

My phone vibrated on the counter. *I miss you.*

I hadn't spoken to Laura in a couple days. Not because I wanted to avoid her, but because I'd been too busy with work. Sometimes the nights were quiet with inactivity, but then there were other nights that lasted days—like this one. *I miss you too.*

Then why aren't you here?

I wished I were there, buried deep between my woman's thighs, but I was stuck on a stiff stool in a quiet bar, waiting for a hit on my life. *I have shit that requires my attention. I'll come when I can.* I would always tell her the truth. If I died tonight, then this would be our last conversation.

You aren't avoiding me because of what I said?

I stared at the question on the screen, feeling her insecurities in the words. *I'm not that kind of man.* It took a lot more than three little words to scare me off. Her feelings didn't intimidate me.

The door to the bar opened—and Silas walked inside.

I tapped my fingers on the counter to get the bartender's attention. "Listen to me carefully. After you make this guy a drink, excuse yourself to the back and don't come out again."

His eyes widened and he stilled, like my words paralyzed him.

"Do you understand?"

"Yes."

Silas came around the corner, a fat smile on his face. "Drinking alone?"

"My favorite way to drink."

He kept a stool between us and slammed his hand on the bar. "Vodka cranberry."

Piss juice.

With shaky hands, the bartender poured the drink, spilled a little on the counter, and then placed it in front of Silas.

"You going to clean that up?" Silas demanded.

"Of course…" He wiped it up with a rag. "I need to get more napkins from the back." He walked off and left us alone.

I drank my scotch and ignored him. "What do you want, Silas?"

He sat on the stool, his body pivoted toward mine. "Who said I want anything?"

"Don't you have work to do?" I'd put him on assignment this week, and he'd clearly chosen to disregard it. I was aware of that, but I pretended not to be.

Silas turned quiet, my comment getting under his skin.

Exactly as I'd intended.

I pivoted on the stool and met his look head on. "So, what's your plan? To shoot me? Who wears a jacket in July?" He had a small pistol in his left pocket, so he could casually slip his hand inside and pull the trigger without me knowing. Oldest trick in the book.

Silas did his best to keep a straight face, but he failed.

"I have a better idea." I tilted my head back and finished off the drink. "Let's do this—man-to-man." I pulled my shirt over my head, revealing my naked torso. There was no bulletproof vest to protect me. I got to my feet, grabbed a beer from behind the counter, and then slammed it down, breaking the bottle until it was just a shard in my hand.

Silas watched me, his hand still on his glass.

In that moment, the door opened, and his backup arrived. Probably thought I'd be dead right now.

"Kill me—and you take it all."

His eyes shifted back and forth.

"Or you can just shoot me like a coward. That sounds more like your style."

That got him on his feet. He grabbed a bottle and slammed it down. Beer and froth poured out, and he had his sharp weapon to take me down.

The other people in the bar hightailed it out of there, heading to the emergency exit to get on the street as quickly as possible.

I kicked aside one of the nearby tables so we'd have room to slice each other apart. I faced him, the bottle gripped in my hand, my heart beating slow and steady. It was a long standoff, the two of us just looking at each other.

Then he lunged, slicing the shard through the air.

I stepped out of the way and immediately ducked, anticipating his next swing. I stayed on the defense, letting him swing and miss time and time again, letting him drain all his energy with this uncoordinated attack.

I evaded him and moved back.

"I'm sick of your shit, Bartholomew."

"That's a shame, because I'm just getting started."

His jaw clenched, and his face tinted red with anger. "You don't deserve our loyalty. You don't give a shit about us."

"Yes, I do."

"Yeah?" He stepped closer, his shirt stained with drops of beer. "Then tell me about John. Who was he?"

I didn't understand the question. "His wife was Johanna. His son—"

"See? You have no fucking idea."

I still didn't understand, and I didn't drop my guard because I knew it was probably a distraction.

"You had no fucking idea that John was my brother—because you don't give a shit about any of us."

I kept a straight face and hid my surprise. No, I didn't know that, and I wasn't sure how I'd forgotten...or maybe

I'd never known. Now it all made sense, his irrational anger, his silent protests.

He lunged at me, swiping the bottle left and right.

I dodged all of the swings—except one.

He sliced me down the arm, and the blood immediately poured.

The sight of red egged him on, and he moved to land a fatal blow.

I ducked the next hit, spun around, and twisted his arm until I slammed it on the table. The bottle flew free.

He screamed and tried to evade my hold, knowing my bottle was going right for his neck.

I threw it against the wall instead, then pinned his arms back before I kicked him in the knees. He fell to the floor, and I pushed him down, getting him flat on his stomach. My boot moved to his head, a warning to keep him still. "If I didn't give a shit about my men, you'd be bleeding out right now."

He breathed hard against the floor, his cheek pressed into the wood.

"I want no more of this." I pulled my boot from his head. "Your betrayal is punishable by death, but I'll spare your life. I'm sorry that I let John die, but now we're even. I know John would want you to accept my mercy and live your life."

He stayed on the floor and continued to breathe hard.

I extended my hand to him.

He continued to lie there, as if struggling to accept the humiliation. Not only had I bested him, but I also had the mercy to spare him. I reminded him exactly why I was in charge, why I'd run the Chasseurs for a decade.

He finally pushed himself up but didn't take my hand.

I withdrew the gesture. "Are we good?"

He wouldn't look directly at me, furious.

I raised my voice. "My mercy has an expiration date, Silas."

"Yes." He finally met my stare. "We're good."

The cut was deep, so I had to get stitches from the doctor on my payroll. It was wrapped in black gauze afterward to keep the wound clean as it healed. I didn't want Laura to see it because she would worry, but it would take at least five days before the wrap was gone, and then there would be a scar underneath—and she would notice that anyway.

I'm on my way. I never asked her permission. If she was mine, then I could be with her whenever I wished. Didn't need to explain a damn thing.

Can't wait to see you.

I arrived fifteen minutes later, entering her apartment without knocking, making myself right at home.

She was in the kitchen—buck naked. She just filled her wineglass and took a drink, sexy tits on display. She wore a cheeky smile, like she enjoyed catching someone like me off guard. "Would you like a drink?"

I slowly walked to her, came around the kitchen island until we were close together.

"Yes." I took the wineglass from her hand and took a drink.

She watched me, her nipples hard from the draft.

I tilted the glass and poured it down her body, watching the rivers glide over her tits and to her stomach. Small pools formed at her feet, and her tits became firmer once the cold liquid caressed her skin.

I lifted her onto the counter and kissed her body, lapping up the wine with my tongue, tasting her skin as well as the bold flavors of the cheap wine. I sucked it off her nipples then made my way down to drink it out of her pierced belly button. Lower I went, drinking it from her thighs.

I tilted her back then poured the wine down her front, watching it drip all the way down to her pussy and onto the floor. I moved to my knees and got wine all over my jeans so I could kiss her, so I could taste the wine with her sweetness.

She moaned when she felt my tongue, squeezing my head with her sexy thighs. "Yes..." She lay back entirely, letting me please her on the kitchen counter, the wine a mess all over the floor.

It took almost no time to push her to the brink, to listen to her moans echo off the ceiling. Making a woman come had never been a challenge, but Laura made it especially easy. I scooped her into my arms and carried her to the bedroom. I laid her on the bed then pulled my shirt over my head.

That was as far as we got before she noticed. "What happened to your arm?"

I removed my bottoms, hoping my nakedness would grab her focus once more. My knees hit the bed, and then I moved up her body, ready to fuck her to tears.

"Bartholomew." She didn't say my name in the sexy way I liked. It was heavy with concern, her focus totally taken out of the moment. "Answer me."

I grabbed the back of her hair and tugged her head back.

She stilled at the aggressive way I handled her.

"Later." I hadn't fucked her in days, and the last thing I cared about was the cat scratch on my arm.

She didn't dare defy me after that.

I folded her underneath me then slid into her slit of heaven. A weight had been lifted from my shoulders, and burying myself between my woman's thighs was exactly how I wanted to celebrate.

I sat at the dining table in just my jeans as I smoked my cigar.

In my t-shirt, she moved about the kitchen, throwing together our dinner. "So?" She'd hardly waited fifteen minutes before her intrusiveness returned.

I took another puff of my cigar and let the smoke rise to the ceiling. "I had a confrontation."

"Obviously." She grabbed the two plates and set them on the table. Our dinner was accompanied by a cheap bottle of wine and a baguette. The money in her bank account should afford her finer things in life, but maybe she didn't appreciate nice things yet. She didn't touch her food and instead stared at me hard, prying for an answer.

"You don't want to hear this story, sweetheart."

"Why not?"

Because it's your fault it happened. "Two of my men died in Florence. One of them had a brother in the Chasseurs—and he wasn't happy that his brother's death was a result of my inadequacy. A lot of my own men distrusted me, didn't respect me. So, he tried to kill me."

Her eagerness quickly evaporated, and to cover the dryness in her throat, she took a drink of her wine. "But you killed him."

"Actually, I spared him. We fought each other with broken bottles. He got my arm, but I got his throat. Instead of killing him, I granted him mercy in order to earn the favor of my men again."

"You aren't worried he might try again?"

I shrugged. "He wouldn't have the support of the men if he did. At that point, it would just be an outside attack, and there would be repercussions. That was his one chance—and he failed."

"How bad is your arm?"

"I needed stitches."

She released a heavy breath. "I'm glad you're alright."

"I'm always alright."

"And I'm sorry...that I've caused you such grief." She didn't meet my gaze, too ashamed.

"I know you are." Finally, there was no resentment. That chapter had been closed.

I put out the cigar, and we ate our dinner quietly. She whipped up chicken Marsala like she'd made it countless times. Her culinary skills weren't extensive, but what she could make was pretty good. She devoured the bread, but I didn't touch it.

With her eyes downcast she said, "It just came out. I wasn't thinking. I'm sorry if I made you uncomfortable, and I'd appreciate it if we just pretended it never happened." She sliced her fork into the tender meat drenched in wine sauce and placed it in her mouth.

It took me a moment to understand her reference. "Alright."

She kept her eyes down as she cut into another piece.

"But I already knew."

Her chin immediately lifted, and her eyes locked on mine.

"Doesn't matter whether you say it or not."

"How-how did you know?"

"Because I can feel it."

20

LAURA

Bartholomew sat on the edge of the bed and pulled on his boots. He began the long process of tightening the laces before he secured them in a knot.

I still wore his shirt, and I wasn't anxious to give it up. "Can you stay?" Now that work had calmed down, I hoped he had more free time to spend with me. We hadn't slept together much, but every time we did, it was magical. I loved seeing his face first thing in the morning.

He looked at me, arms on his knees. "I can stay until you fall asleep." He'd just woken up a couple hours ago, so he wouldn't be able to sleep beside me and have breakfast in the morning.

So I took the offer. "Alright."

He untied his boots and slipped them off before he stripped down to his boxers.

I removed his shirt so he could wear it when he left.

We got into bed, nearly naked, and that strong arm wrapped around me and pulled me close. Sealed in his warmth and his manly scent, I was happy. I stared at his face beside me, treasured the sight of those beautiful eyes as I felt the fullness in my heart. My fingers lightly felt his chest and his neck, feeling the tight cords underneath his skin.

His eyes were on me, hardly blinking.

"Can I ask you something?" I whispered, feeling brave.

His eyes shifted back and forth between mine. "Yes."

"Would you ever want something more than this…?" I'd fallen head over heels for this man and wanted a lifetime at his side. I wanted his mornings and his nights. I wanted to be his wife, the mother of his children. But would he ever want those things?

"When you laid down the rules for this relationship, you made it very clear *more* was off the table."

"That was before I fell in love with you." *Or admitted that I was in love with you.*

His eyes remained steady, unaffected by the romantic confession. "Define more."

"Move in together, maybe?" I asked hopefully.

"You want to live with me?"

"Yeah…I would love that."

"Alright."

What…? "Alright what?"

"I asked you to move in with me, and you said yes."

I'd missed it, assuming it was all hypothetical. "Really?"

"Really."

"So, you do want more…" I felt the smile move on to my lips. "It's kinda crazy to ask a woman to live with you when you don't love her."

"Who said I don't?"

The smile left my face, and a tightness moved to my chest. I suddenly felt like I wasn't getting enough air, like I was on the verge of a panic attack, but then it passed instantaneously and I felt a joyful calm. "I didn't know you felt that way."

"Not the kind of guy to say such things. But I will say that I've loved you far longer than you've loved me." He said it with a hard face, without an ounce of emotion. "I would have let you die if I didn't."

His words were beautiful in the beginning but had a horrible aftertaste. I'd chosen my father, a man who would have killed me, over the man who loved me enough to sacrifice his whole world.

He must have seen the distress in my face because he said, "It's in the past. Let it go."

"It's hard…"

"I have." His fingers slid into my hair, and he kissed me on the forehead. "I've forgiven you. Forgive yourself."

I didn't have a lot of things to pack.

The furniture would be donated because Bartholomew's apartment was already furnished. I'd only been there a few times and spent most of my time in his bedroom, but I could tell all his belongings were designer-level and custom-made. My table from IKEA had no business there.

So it was just my clothes.

And I had *a lot* of clothes.

I began the process of putting everything into boxes as they still hung on the hangers. I went through my keepsakes, old photo albums of my family when life was good. My mom was beautiful and my dad seemed happy.

But who knows if he'd ever been happy a day in his life.

My apartment door opened, and heavy boots thudded on the floor.

"In here." I sat on the bedroom floor, my stuff scattered everywhere, a stack of fold-up boxes leaning against the wall.

Bartholomew rounded the corner, dressed in his signature black, and looked at me from the doorway.

"I hope you have room in your closet for all these clothes."

"I do."

"Good. Because I'm not leaving anyone behind."

The corner of his lips quirked up in a smile before he took a seat on the floor, leaning against the wall, his arms resting on his knees. "When do you think you'll be ready?"

"In a couple days. It's hard to get anything done when I'm at work all day."

"Do you want to keep any of the furniture?"

"No. It would look hideous in your apartment." But it was nice that he offered.

"Hungry?"

"You know I'm always hungry."

His lips quirked up again before he got to his feet. "Where do you want to go?"

"Something casual." I was wearing jeans and a t-shirt, something I didn't care about while I worked in the apartment. "I don't exactly look my best." I wasn't even wearing makeup because I would just sweat it off.

"Really? I didn't even notice."

We went to a café that served sandwiches and coffee, and after we ordered our food and carried it to the table, we sat across from each other. I could drink coffee all day, every day, so I didn't shy away from having an espresso in the evening. Bartholomew ordered a coffee because it was morning for him.

Our relationship had been different ever since he'd told me how he felt.

That he loved me.

I'd been so lonely these last seven years, and that loneliness had reached a breaking point when my father betrayed me. Without a family, I felt like I was in limbo, never belonging anywhere, never being missed because there was no one to notice I was gone. But now, everything was different.

I felt complete. I felt like I belonged. I felt like...I had a family.

He was everything I needed.

He held the sandwich in a single hand, his elbow on the table, his black coffee steaming. He stuck out here, not because of all the black he wore, but because he was so insanely good-looking. He stuck out in every room that had people. "What is it, sweetheart?"

"Sorry?" I realized I was holding my sandwich without taking a bite. I just stared at him, like a weirdo. "I was just thinking..."

"About?"

"Um..." A lot of thoughts had transpired in the past minute, but I didn't share any of them. "I don't want to be one of those women who obsesses over the future, but...does *more* include marriage? Because...I'd like to marry you someday." He was a hard man to read, and unless I explicitly asked him for information, I wouldn't know the truth.

"Am I the kind of man you'd want to marry?"

"Yes." I said it without hesitation, without doubt.

"Because your previous concerns are still valid."

He was a dangerous man living in a dangerous world—and that meant I was vulnerable. It would always weigh in the back of my mind. "I know you'll always keep me safe."

His reaction was subtle, but it was enough to show how much that meant to him.

"I know you'll always protect me." I meant those words, because I would never consider a life with him if I didn't.

He wasn't what I'd wanted in the beginning, but I knew I would never love another man the way I loved him. I wanted him for the rest of my life.

"I'm open to marriage—someday."

It was a dream come true, and I should have just left it alone, but I wanted to know. "And kids?"

His mood dropped at the question. "You should already know the answer to that."

"You said you would never tell me you loved me or ask me to marry you—but that changed."

"Only because you made it clear you didn't want those things—not because I didn't want to. You think I get irrationally jealous over a lesser man just for the hell of it? You think I demanded to be your man because I'm a possessive asshole? No, it was because I was in love with you, Laura."

Our history had been rewritten with those words.

"But kids—I won't change my mind about that."

God, it hurt.

"It would be irresponsible to have them anyway, given what I do. What kind of parents would we be if we thought that environment was appropriate? You know that better than anyone after all the shit you've been through."

"Well...in that scenario, you would be retired."

His eyes stilled like I'd just insulted him. "I'm annoyed by this conversation, but I realize it's necessary before you move in. So let me be absolutely clear in this. There's no scenario in which we have children. There's no scenario in which I suddenly decide fatherhood is right for me. Not everyone is meant to be a parent—and certainly not me."

"Not even to be with the woman you love...?"

His answer was immediate. "No."

"Can I ask you something?"

He gave an audible sigh, like this conversation was causing him a headache.

"Is it because you don't want children or because you deem yourself inadequate to raise them?"

"Both."

"I understand what you went through with your parents—"

"You don't. Just as I'll never understand how it feels for your father to look you in the eye and threaten to kill you. You can analyze my past all you want, but it's not going to change my future. My line dies with me. If the two of us aren't enough for you, then perhaps this is the end of the road for us."

I couldn't imagine my life without children—but I couldn't imagine my life without him either. "Is this something you would reconsider in the future—"

"No."

"You might feel differently after you've been married for a while—"

"No."

"Bartholomew—"

"*Laura.* The answer is no. It'll always be no. I trust you enough to know that you wouldn't trap me into it. And if you did, I would financially support you, but I would never spend a single moment with that child."

I was stunned into silence.

Our food and coffee were abandoned. Our joy had evaporated.

I had a difficult decision ahead of me. But when I looked down that road, the only face I saw was his. My heart beat for this man, and it would never beat for anyone else. If I found someone else, they would always be my second choice, and that seemed cruel. While I wanted children, I wanted them with someone I loved, and to have them with someone I loved less…didn't make sense. I believed Bartholomew was capable of change and growth because I'd witnessed it with my own eyes. I believed there was a chance he would change his mind someday, but he wasn't ready for that today. "Okay."

"Okay what?" he asked, his voice still a bit cold.

"I want to be with you—no matter what our future looks like."

He stared at me for a long time, the hardness slowly softening, like waves turning rock to sand. The silence continued as he studied my face, taking me in with a new depth. "You're certain?"

"I'm certain I'll never love anyone else the way I love you."

His heavy body moved on top of mine, six-foot-something of manly perfection, and his narrow hips squeezed between my soft thighs until he sank inside me. Inch after inch filled me until his big dick had fully claimed me. Dark eyes were locked on to mine, and he started to rock, taking it slow without my having to ask.

I moved my hands up his muscled back and into his hair, digging into the thick strands, rocking my hips back into him, feeling a deeper connection than I'd ever felt before. Our bodies came closer to each other, and we writhed together, our breaths short, our moans loud. My face rested against his cheek as I clung to him. "I love you..." My nails dug into his back as I got lost in the moment, free to say what was in my heart without judgment or rejection. I said it again and again, not needing to hear him say it back.

Because I could feel it.

Most of the boxes were stacked in the living room. My furniture was still there because Bartholomew said he would have one of his guys take care of the removal. I stood in front of the closet and looked at my remaining clothes, the stuff in the very back, outfits I hardly ever wore. Should I take them or donate them?

I hadn't worn them in a year, so I guessed I should give them away.

The door opened and footsteps sounded.

"I'm almost done. Just a couple more things." My heart always skipped a beat when he dropped by unannounced, walking into the apartment because he was always welcome wherever I was.

His boots thudded against the hardwood as he approached the doorway. Then he came into view, wearing blue jeans and a gray t-shirt.

And then I realized it wasn't Bartholomew.

It was someone else.

Someone who grinned at me like a psychopath.

"Expecting someone else?" He leaned against the doorframe and crossed his arms. Then he looked me up and down slowly, his eyes violating my fully clothed body. "This is going to be fun."

21

BARTHOLOMEW

The SUV pulled up to the building, and we all filed out of the car.

My phone rang, and if it weren't Laura calling me, I wouldn't have answered. "Busy right now. I'll call you back."

"Hopefully she's still alive by then." The man's voice was like nails against a chalkboard on my ears. I stopped midstep, and my surroundings faded to nothing. I pictured Silas grinning like a goddamn clown.

All the guys stopped and looked at me.

I didn't have time to make a plan before I responded. He'd caught me off guard—and I had to think quickly. "What do you want, Silas?"

"Right down to business. I expected questions. I expected threats."

I didn't play games when it came to my woman.

"I killed all your watchmen then walked right into her apartment. You should tell your girl to lock her door."

I kept my voice steady. "What do you want, Silas?"

"You're no fun, Bartholomew."

"I granted you mercy—and this is how you repay me."

"It wasn't mercy. It was a fucking PR stunt."

A successful PR stunt. "There's no scenario in which you survive this. Even if you kill me, they'll kill you."

"We'll see."

"Make your demands."

"All it takes is a woman to make you cooperative... Wish I'd known that sooner."

"Make your demands." I couldn't keep my patience much longer.

His smile was in his voice. "Come to the apartment —alone."

"And then you'll let her go?"

"I'll see how I feel when you get here."

I ran down the hallway and burst into the apartment, the apartment where I'd fallen for the daughter of my enemy. It started off as meaningless fucks in lingerie but turned into quiet conversations over home-cooked meals and cheap wine. Instead of seeing a beautiful woman, I saw a woman with a soul identical to mine.

Now it was a nightmare.

The men rushed me, patting me down to check for guns and knives. Silas leaned against the kitchen island and watched. My eyes searched for Laura, but she was nowhere to be found.

I pushed them off when they were done. "Where is she?"

He nodded toward the bedroom.

"You've got me. Now let her go."

"I will, but there's something I want to do first."

"*Bartholomew!*" Her frantic voice came from the bedroom.

I ran down the hallway, and when one of the guys grabbed me, I threw him against the wall so hard he was knocked out cold. The scene in the bedroom made my blood run cold. Laura was tied up on the bed—buck naked.

No.

She pulled on the ropes for dear life, dried tears on her ghost-white cheeks.

"Tie him down."

The men jumped on me, and I fought with everything I had, throwing one guy off and immediately jabbing another in the eye. I never pulled those kinds of stunts and played dirty, but they'd played dirty first.

A gun cocked.

Silas pressed the barrel of the gun into her temple. "Sit."

No.

Laura panted, new tears coming to her eyes. "I'd rather die…"

Silas gestured to the chair. "Sit."

I had a choice—an impossible one.

I moved to the chair.

Laura screamed. "No! Let him kill me!"

A thunderstorm of pain ripped through me, but I had to keep a straight face, had to remain calm. If I lost it, she would have no way to get through this. I dropped into the chair, and then my wrists were secured behind the wooden chair they'd pulled from the dining table. "Silas, she has nothing to do with this."

"Yeah? She's the reason my brother died, isn't she?"

My breaths shortened, but I did my best to keep them subtle. "I'm the reason your brother died. I was the one who made the choice. Punish me."

"I will, Bartholomew. I will punish you where it hurts." He set the gun on the nightstand then pulled his shirt over his head.

Laura fought with all her strength to break through the ropes. Her naked body lifted up and down, rocking the headboard. She screamed through her tears. "Don't you fucking touch me!"

I'd seen some serious shit, but this was scarring.

I subtly checked the rope around my wrists, seeing that they'd made a double knot I couldn't untie within a reasonable amount of time. My ankles were secured too. Otherwise, I could throw my body right at them.

His shoes and pants were off, and now he was naked.

And hard.

Laura continued to fight, to move her body away from him as his knees hit the bed.

My hands yanked against the rope, but it was no use.

"Bartholomew!" She screamed for me to help her—*but I couldn't.*

He forced her onto her stomach so he could take her from behind, her ankles together and her wrists secured above her head. Her screams were muffled as her face was pressed into the comforter. Then he raised his hand and spanked her ass—hard. "That's a fine piece of—"

I let out a scream and pulled every muscle in my body at once. Just like with a mother who lifted a car off her child, the adrenaline increased my strength, and I shattered the wooden chair into two separate pieces.

"Silas!"

I forced my back into the first man and made him slam into the wall. When the next guy came, I spun and struck the chair against him. Then I did something I'd never done before and threw my arms over my head, nearly popping my shoulders out of the sockets, and finished off the next one who came for me—while my ankles were still locked together.

Silas lunged for the gun on the nightstand.

I jumped forward, over the corner of the bed, and pushed the gun off the surface before he could reach it. It landed on the floor closer to me, and I grabbed it first. Then I aimed it at his terrified face—and fired.

Again.

And again.

Once the gunshots were over, it was quiet.

Except for Laura—who sobbed.

I yanked the rope free from my ankles and got to her as quickly as I could. I untied her wrists and ankles then pulled my shirt over my head and dropped it onto her exposed body, even though everyone except us was dead.

She moved into my chest and sobbed.

"It's over, sweetheart." My arms locked around her body like steel bars, and I held her. My chin rested on her head, and I felt the tears build in my eyes. They were hot tears, tears I hadn't felt in over a decade. I didn't let them fall. I blinked several times, forced them to dry, and pretended it hadn't happened. "I'm here...I'm right here."

22

LAURA

I didn't speak for days.

Bartholomew relocated me to his apartment, and I spent my time barricaded in his bedroom, which was bigger than my entire apartment. It had its own sitting room with a TV, had a bathtub as big as a hot tub, a balcony that had a beautiful view of the city.

His butler brought all my meals, and I ate at the dining table, sometimes alone, sometimes with him there to watch me. I hardly looked at Bartholomew, and I wore his baggy clothes at all times.

He never left me.

Sometimes he would work from the couch, his laptop on his knees, taking phone calls throughout the day and night. But he never left the room. Whenever I showered, he never stepped into the bathroom, respecting my privacy.

He never spoke to me. Didn't ask me a single question. He was the most intuitive man I knew, understanding I wasn't ready to talk without having to hear me say it. He was patient, giving me everything I needed without instruction.

Finally, I found the words. "What happened...?" I sat across from him at the dining table, my spoon sitting in the bowl of soup I had hardly touched.

His elbows were on the table and he was about to take another bite, but he abandoned his utensils and his appetite to look at me straight on. "He's the one who gave me the cut." He moved his left arm, which now had a long scar that almost reached his elbow. "I should have killed him. I'll never make that mistake again."

"Why me...?"

His eyes dropped. "He knows I'm not afraid of pain or death. Hurting someone important to me is the only way to stress my pain receptors. Otherwise...I feel nothing." He looked at me again. "I'm so sorry." He'd probably never apologized for anything in his life, but he said the words with pure sincerity. "It'll never happen again."

"You can't guarantee that."

His eyes hardened. "Yes, I can."

"Then why did it happen in the first place?"

"Because you lived elsewhere. If you lived under my roof, you would be untouchable."

"Except when I leave to go to work or the gym…"

He took a breath, subtle restraint on his frustration. "I have men protecting me within a mile radius of every place I go. When you're my woman, I would give you the exact same protection. Snipers in buildings. Men working at coffee carts with assault rifles stowed underneath. Eyes would be on you—always."

"But this was one of your men. Not an outsider. So if that happens again, no one will know I'm in danger."

He released another breath. "Sweetheart, I'll work out the logistics later. But I will make it my priority to keep you safe. My number one priority—always."

I recognized this feeling of numbness because I'd felt it before—when I was raped. It took years of therapy to recover, and now I was back to ground zero. It was more traumatizing than before, but it was a repeated offense. I'd known what would happen before it happened, like it was all in slow motion. "Bartholomew, I can't do this. I love you so much...but I can't do this." I had no tears because I was incapable of feeling anything right now.

"Laura." Now his voice was as hard as his eyes. "I will always protect you."

"You didn't protect me then."

"Nothing happened. I stopped it from happening, and I killed all of them—"

"But barely. You didn't have a plan. That chair could have been made out of metal, and the outcome would have been very different—"

"I would have found a way, Laura." He tried to silence me with his angry eyes, but it wouldn't work.

"Nothing happened...?" I asked, my voice quiet. "They held me down and stripped off all my clothes." I kept my voice steady, but it wanted to shake. My eyes burned into his, wanting him to understand how horrible it was. "They flicked my nipples until I cried."

He struggled to keep a straight face, but his shortened breaths gave away his anger.

"They pissed on me—"

"*Stop*." He caved, his eyes severing contact.

"Don't say nothing happened."

"But *that* didn't happen." He lifted his chin and looked at me again. "I'm not dismissing what you went through...but I stopped the worst of it. I protected you exactly as I promised—and I will protect you better once you're under my roof."

Being with the love of my life wasn't an equal trade-off, not for the risk. "You're a very powerful man, Bartholomew. During our time together, I've come to appreciate just how majestic that power really is. But when you're at the top, all eyes are on you. I'm your one and only weakness—and I'll live the rest of my life with a target on my back."

His stare had hardened again, all his walls up.

"I can't do it." I'd be scared every single day, wondering *when* it would happen, not *if*.

A heavy silence filled the dead space between us. Bartholomew was mute, lacking an argument to combat the truth of my words. He eventually looked away, his eyes on the window that showed the buildings across the street. It stayed that way for a long time—the two of us accepting the end of our relationship.

"Unless…"

After a beat, he looked at me again.

"Unless…you walked away from it all."

His breaths were slow and steady, his eyes hard as concrete.

If he were willing to do it, he would have suggested it on his own. I knew his answer before he gave it, but a part of me irrationally hoped he would make a different choice if I asked.

Then his eyes dropped—and that was the end of it.

How could that answer hurt so much when I already knew it was coming? How could the expected catch me by surprise? How could I…feel so broken? "It's always been my dream to have a family…to replace what I lost, but I was willing to give that up for you. But you aren't willing to make an equal sacrifice for me." I said the words slowly, talking myself through the horrible realization.

He kept his eyes down—like a coward.

"Goodbye, Bartholomew."

When I entered my apartment, I felt sick to my stomach, and not just because I'd lost the love of my life. Painful memories washed over me, the echoes of my screams, flashbacks from a horror movie.

I looked at the pile of boxes I'd have to unpack.

But I didn't have the energy.

I walked into my bedroom, seeing the remains of that moment, pee stains on the sheets.

I shut the door and walked to the couch—and went straight to sleep.

I did that on and off for days, never unpacking, never stepping into that bedroom. I raided the cabinets in search of food during the rare times I had an appetite. Life passed with painstaking slowness. There wasn't anything to look forward to in life—except feeling better.

A knock sounded on the door.

I didn't expect it to be Bartholomew. He would never change his mind—not now, not ever—because nothing was more important than his power and money.

Not even me.

I looked through the peephole and saw a man I didn't know. I decided not to answer it.

"Bartholomew sent me." He must have seen my shadow under the door or heard my breaths. "Wanted me to give you something."

I opened the door and came face-to-face with the messenger, not caring that I looked like hell with unwashed hair and old clothes.

He gave me a large envelope, the kind that contained full-page documents. I took it from him and opened it at the kitchen counter.

A set of keys fell out.

The envelope held a bunch of documents—and I quickly realized it was a deed to property in my name.

I read the note he'd included.

Laura,

You deserve a better apartment. You deserve a better family. You deserve a better man than me. Start a new life. Fall in love with a good man. Have a family. Have everything that I'm unable to give you—and forget about me.

The address was written below his signature.

I read his letter again, and it hurt as much the second time as the first. When we'd broken up the first time, I'd always believed there was a chance we would get back together. My heart still beat for him, hoping, dreaming...

But not this time.

This time...it was really over.

It was an apartment I could never afford, not if I worked thirty years and saved every single cent. It was in a prime location in Paris, with a doorman out front, a private parking garage, and it was two stories with at least three thousand square feet. And it was fully furnished, with chic decorations and high-end furniture.

The place had to be worth five million...at least.

In the note, he'd explained the property taxes would be covered indefinitely, so I never had to worry about a bill I wouldn't be able to pay.

I shouldn't accept such a ridiculous gift, but I couldn't live in my old apartment anymore. I couldn't sleep on the couch and keep the bedroom door closed. I couldn't be haunted by the horrible things that had happened there…and the good things too.

I needed a fresh start, a place that hadn't been infected by Bartholomew's presence, a place that would be free of his ghost.

23

BARTHOLOMEW

Someone shook me. "Bartholomew?"

I lay there, unable to open my eyes.

"He's been like this all day," Bleu said. "You think I should call an ambulance?"

Someone shook me again, this time harder. Then they slapped me across the face. "Asshole, wake up."

I recognized that voice.

"I've never seen him like this," Bleu said.

"I have." He slapped me again, even harder than the last.

My eyes finally snapped open, and I almost rolled off the couch. "Hit me again and…" The world spun, and I almost slid to the hardwood floor.

His hand caught me. "You'll what?" Benton asked. "Slur me to death?" He forced me back onto the couch. "Alcohol poisoning. Call Maurice."

Bleu took off.

"What the fuck are you doing?" Benton demanded.

The migraine kicked in as I became more conscious. "Jesus…"

"Are you trying to kill yourself? Put the gun in your mouth and pull the trigger next time." He slapped me again.

"Fuck, I'm awake!"

"That one was just for the hell of it." He lifted me and forced me to sit upright against the couch. "Your head will feel better."

I sat there, slouched against the couch, my head throbbing. The bottles and glasses were on the coffee table where I'd left them.

Minutes later, my doctor arrived and stuck an IV in my arm. He hydrated me as well as pumped me with some drugs. It took a couple minutes, but I started to feel better, though I'd never felt so weak.

Benton sat on the other couch, dogging me with a hateful look.

"You didn't have to come."

"Apparently I'm the only man you trust, and I don't even work with you anymore. Pretty fucking sad."

"Or you could take it as a compliment..."

"No. It's just a nuisance."

My head rested on the back of the cushion, and I looked at the ceiling. I was still drunk, so after a couple minutes, I forgot Benton was there.

"Are you going to tell me what happened?"

My eyes opened again, coming back into consciousness. "Hard day."

"The last time you had a *hard day* was when you went to kill your parents but changed your mind when you realized they had more kids and never bothered to look for you."

"Good times..."

"What happened with Laura?"

"Why do you assume it's her?"

"Because she's the only one who has the power to hurt you like this."

I closed my eyes again, my eyelids suddenly heavy. "It wasn't her."

"Then who?"

"Me." My eyes opened again, and I shifted my body farther up the couch. "It was me..." I'd hated myself a lot over the years, but never at this intensity.

"What did you do?"

"I asked her to give up her dream to be with me—but I wouldn't do the same for her." I was such a fucking asshole. All the fight had left my body when she'd said those words...because they were true. I didn't deserve her. I'd never deserved her. I'd walked into her shop and ruined her goddamn life. What if I had just kept walking? What if I hadn't tainted her life with my bullshit?

Benton was quiet for a long time.

The words absorbed into my skin—and hurt even more.

"You broke up with her?"

"She left me." I told him what happened with Silas. "I didn't protect her, Benton. And she's right... There's no guarantee I'll be able to protect her in the future. She made the right choice. I should have made it for her."

He was quiet again, processing all of that. "You love this woman, Bartholomew."

I raised my arm with the IV in my vein. "Clearly."

"But you're going to choose this life over her?"

"It's a life sentence, Benton. You don't just walk away—"

"That's a bullshit excuse, and you know it."

I directed my gaze elsewhere, keeping Benton in my peripheral so I wouldn't have to see the disappointment on his face.

"You're making a mistake."

"Maybe I am."

"Then fix it before it's too late."

"I can't."

"Why?"

I said nothing.

"*Why?*" he repeated. "You have more money than you know what to do with. Walk away—and be with the woman you love. Enjoy your life."

I ignored him.

"Bartholomew, help me understand—"

"Because I'm nothing without it." I looked at him head on. "I'm just a man. That's it."

His voice turned quiet, approaching the topic with gentleness. "That's exactly what she wants, Bartholomew—"

"She wants the man she met. The man who terrifies people. The man who owns these streets and everyone in them. I'll just be a fucking nobody with a lot of money. Weak. Boring. Forgettable. And then what happens? She leaves me. She leaves me—and I'm left with nothing." I probably wouldn't have said any of that if I weren't still drunk, with painkillers saturating my system. "She'll leave like everyone else. I've built the Chasseurs from nothing. It's always been there for me, always been the place I belong, my purpose in life. I work nonstop because I enjoy it—"

"Because you've never had anything else or anyone else to spend time with. All you have is work because you've never slowed down to enjoy life. You've never enjoyed life because you don't know how. You don't know how to celebrate Christmas. There's no one in your life who even knows your birthday. Not even me, your closest friend—"

"You want to sing happy birthday to me and watch me blow out some fucking candles? Fuck that."

Benton hesitated. "It's what makes your life rich, it fills all the emptiness, it hides the loneliness."

"You're a therapist now?" I snapped.

"No, but I know exactly how you feel. Been there, done that. Remember?"

I looked away.

"All things come to an end, Bartholomew. It's your time to walk off the stage. Not in defeat, but victory."

I still didn't look at him.

"Don't lose her over this."

"Even if I did…I can't give her what she wants."

"Which is?"

"Kids. I fucking *hate* kids."

Benton didn't say anything.

"I'm not having a kid just to neglect them. Just to hate them. Just to regret their very existence."

"That's not how it would be."

"Yes, it would."

"Just because your parents—"

"Shut the fuck up." I looked at him again. "I'm done with this bullshit conversation." Maybe the booze had started to wear off a bit, because I no longer felt loose. I felt rigid, hard, impenetrable. "I'd be an idiot to give up everything for a single person. If she wants to be with me, it has to be my way—and that's it. She made her choice, and she made the right one."

"So you're saying you only want to be in a relationship if they risk everything and you risk nothing?"

"Yes."

Benton's eyes narrowed. "So you don't trust her."

"I don't trust anyone, Benton."

24

LAURA

A month had come and gone.

I went to work then returned to my apartment like clockwork. When I was home, I continued to work on my laptop because I had nothing else to occupy my mind. In all that time, Bartholomew had never texted me.

I didn't text him.

It was a clean break. A breakup we both wanted.

Sometimes I wondered if he'd already slept with someone new, but then I forced myself to stop thinking about it. It didn't matter whether he did or not. It didn't matter whether I did or not.

It was over.

I knew I should try dating again, put myself out there and resume a regular life. The sooner I did normal things, the sooner I would feel normal. Maybe I'd meet a nice guy and that would spark excitement again.

But that wasn't enough to make me try. I didn't sign up for any dating apps. Didn't go out in the hope of meeting someone. I stayed home—alone.

I'd just finished dinner when someone knocked on the door.

They had to check in with the doorman first, so they must have said the right thing to make it up to my floor. I looked in the peephole and saw a handsome man I didn't know. I'd become a paranoid person, carrying a Taser in my purse, checking my surroundings at all times, never leaving the office after dark. So I didn't open the door.

"Benton," he said into the peephole. "I'm a friend of Bartholomew's."

I recognized the name, and that was what made me open the door. I hadn't heard his name in a month, and I suspected I would never hear his name again. "Is he alright?"

He was in a gray t-shirt and dark jeans. He had the bluest eyes I'd ever seen. A hard face. A wedding ring was on his left hand. "Can I come in?"

I opened the door wider and watched him enter my apartment. "Is he okay?" I repeated.

"He's fine." He turned to face me, the two of us having our conversation in my entryway. "I'll make this quick... don't want to disturb your life."

My life of being alone. "Okay."

"I just wanted you to know I did my best to save him from himself. But no matter what I said or how I said it, he wouldn't budge."

"I don't understand your meaning."

"I tried to convince him that he'd made the wrong choice. That he should walk away from everything and have a quiet life with you."

"Oh..."

"And if it helps, he's been miserable. I mean...more than miserable."

"No, that doesn't help at all," I said coldly. "I wouldn't want him if someone had to talk him into it."

He slid his hands into his pockets.

"Thanks for trying…I guess."

"He has his demons. He has his issues. I just wish he were strong enough to leave all that in the past and take a chance."

I didn't quite understand what that meant, but I had a good idea. "Bartholomew isn't the kind of man that changes. He won't change for me. He won't change for anyone. And that's fine, because that's who he is."

He watched me for a while. "You're taking this breakup a lot better than he is."

"I'm really not. I've just come to accept that it's over. That's it for the best. He either would have had to make sacrifices to be with me or I would have had to make sacrifices to be with him, and that's not how a relationship should be." The fact that we'd had no contact whatsoever made it easier too. If I saw his handsome face, it would probably evoke all the feelings I'd worked so hard to bury. "It's over. And it's okay that it's over."

I was at the shop, taking in a dress to my client's exact measurements. It was the end of summer, so the tourists had finally started to dissipate, but the heat lingered. It'd been a few weeks since Benton had paid me an unexpected visit.

I wished he hadn't—because it only made me feel worse.

I wanted nothing to do with his world.

I didn't want any reminder that our relationship had ever been real.

My phone started to ring, and I almost didn't notice because my thoughts were so deep. I thought of our first kiss. I remembered the way he looked at me from across the room. I remembered the way he made me feel loved without ever saying the actual words. A series of images and emotions flashed by.

Then the phone caught my attention.

It was Victor.

Bartholomew disappeared from my mind, and I wondered if my father had suffered from a heart attack or a stroke. There was no other reason Victor would call me. My father was either dead or in the hospital.

I took the call. "Victor, what's going on?"

He whispered, like he was in a compromised position. "I have less than thirty seconds, so just listen."

Oh fuck.

"Leonardo just called a hit on Bartholomew. We're about to strike his apartment. I don't know why I decided to tell you this, but I thought you should know."

25

BARTHOLOMEW

I'd just stepped out of my gym when I heard it.

Thud.

My eyes lifted to the floor above mine.

It sounded like a body.

I pulled out my phone and checked the alarm system. It was disabled. The panic button hadn't been pushed. But the system said the front door had opened—and it was still open. I fired off a quick text to Bleu. *There's been a hit on my apartment. Bring backup.* I slid the phone into my pocket then stepped back into the gym. A rifle with extra rounds was stowed underneath one of the machines. A bulletproof vest was secured under another.

I strapped the vest to my bare chest then poked my head out into the hallway with the rifle in my hands.

Thud.

They'd made it past my security. Prevented my staff from hitting the panic button. And now they combed my apartment, silently taking out my men one by one in the hope of catching me off guard in my bedroom.

I would normally be asleep at this time of day, but sleep didn't come easy for me anymore. I moved down the hallway and scanned the rooms, looking for my first victim. I approached the first one from behind. With a vest strapped to his chest and dressed in all black, he wore nothing distinguishable to identify his boss. I slammed the butt of my gun into the back of his head then caught him before he collapsed. I dragged him into an empty bedroom and left him on the rug.

Thud.

My apartment contained twelve of my men altogether, and I had no idea how many they'd already gotten. The fact that not a single shot had been fired told me none of my guys had the slightest idea what was happening.

I was on my own—until Bleu showed up with backup.

The best thing I could do was stay hidden until Bleu got there.

Twenty minutes came and went, and nothing happened.

Bleu must be dead. I texted other guys, and help was coming, but I'd wasted more time than I could afford.

Then Laura called me.

Out of the fucking blue.

I couldn't answer it, so I switched the phone to silent.

Footsteps grew louder.

"He's in here."

I ducked into a room and pressed against the wall.

"Bleu says he hasn't left."

The shock was so harsh I forgot to breathe.

Bleu.

He'd fucked me.

I was trapped with god knew how many men, and I only had minutes, maybe seconds, before they found me. I could have taken the opportunity to speak to the person who actually mattered before I was shot—but I'd ignored her call.

The footsteps grew louder.

"Check all the rooms. He's hiding somewhere—like a coward."

I recognized that voice. Just took me a second.

Leonardo.

Fucking Leonardo.

I moved into the hallway and fired, ready to kill him first so he wouldn't have the pleasure of watching me die. I sprayed bullets everywhere, taking down the men in the front. I spun around and fired in the opposite direction, but I wasn't quick enough. A knife dug deep into my side, so much more painful than a superficial bullet wound. I was knocked off-balance—and then I fell.

"He's down."

I reached for the gun to shoot the first one in the face, but it was knocked away.

It was Lucas.

The man I hated second most.

He sneered, and he twisted the knife with mirth. "Doesn't feel good, does it?"

The butt of a gun hit me in the back of the head—and I was out.

I didn't know how long I was out for, but it couldn't have been more than a few minutes because I was on the ground floor of my apartment, in the center of the grand entryway where one of the tables had been.

My shirt was gone, and I was bleeding everywhere.

I pushed myself up on my elbows and ignored the screams I wanted to share.

"Good morning, sunshine." Leonardo stood there, dressed in all black, a false smile plastered on his face. "Glad you could join us."

He would draw this out as long as I was alive. That's what I would have done.

The room was full of a dozen of his men, all holding guns. I was on my own, bleeding out, weaponless. My eyes turned to the man in the corner who didn't belong there.

Bleu.

If I'd had a gun in my hand, he'd be the first to go.

He avoided eye contact.

Coward.

Victor was there too, standing behind Leonardo. His voice was devoid of emotion, unlike the rest of the guys.

"Get on with it." There was no way out except with a bullet in my head, so the sooner I made that happen, the sooner this shit would be over.

"Get on with it?" Leonardo stepped forward, breaking out from his line of men. "You ostracized me from my own dealers and squeezed me out of my own business. No, I'm in absolutely no rush, Bartholomew."

"I hate to rain on your parade, but I'll probably bleed out before you can really enjoy yourself. Lucas blew his load too quick. I bet that happens with Catherine too."

Lucas launched forward and pulled the knife out of the sheath.

Victor grabbed him and yanked him back.

"You fucked me, Bartholomew," Leonardo said. "Now I've fucked you. No one is coming to your rescue. They're no longer loyal to you."

"Because I saved *your* daughter."

"You shouldn't have gotten involved with her in the first place. That was low."

"I was involved with her because I loved her. And I still do."

Leonardo hesitated, but it was within the span of a blink, and then he was back to normal. "I hope you don't think I'll spare you on her account. My wife was raped, but I still put our business relationship first."

"And they say chivalry is dead…"

Leonardo stepped forward again. "You won't be laughing when I bust each of your kneecaps."

"Well, you better do it now because I won't be around much longer." I felt my body slip away. It was a slow descent, but it was coming, getting faster all the while.

A scream erupted outside, and that was enough to make us all look.

The door flew open, and Laura ran inside.

No.

Her eyes locked on mine, and she immediately shed tears. "No! Stop this!"

Now I lost my cool, because I couldn't keep it together with her in the room. "Victor, take her out of here."

She pushed a guy aside and tried to run to me.

Victor snatched her and pulled her back.

Leonardo was ice-cold. "She can watch if she wants."

"Please." She fought Victor's hold. "Dad…please."

The name didn't pull on his heartstrings at all. He faced me again and pulled out his gun.

"Stop!"

I couldn't think about her now. There was nothing I could do but die with honor. I didn't look at her because it would be too hard for me—and too hard for her.

Leonardo raised his gun and pointed it at me—and then blood sprayed from his skull. The gunshot echoed off the walls in the grand entryway. Another bullet fired, and he toppled to the floor.

Laura pressed the gun to Victor's head next. "Leave—or I'll shoot him next."

All the men remained still, their dead boss on the floor.

"*Leave!*" She slammed the gun into Victor's head.

They finally moved, filing out the front door.

Victor stood there with his hands in the air.

When the last one was out the door, Laura released him. "Help me!" She sprinted to me where I lay on the floor. "Get up."

It took a moment to look away from Leonardo, to process his unexpected death.

"Get up, Bartholomew!"

I tried, but I slipped on my own blood.

"Victor!"

He slid his gun into the back of his jeans and walked toward us.

She had one of my arms over her neck.

To my surprise, he grabbed the other arm and helped me to my feet.

Bleu came forward. "Bartholomew—"

"Shoot this motherfucker." I reached for Victor's gun.

Bleu raised his hands. "He said he would kill Benton and his family if I didn't cooperate."

I stilled.

"I did what I thought you'd want."

"Come on, help us," Laura said.

Bleu took her place, and the guys carried me outside.

Leonardo's men were outside, but no shots were fired, probably because they were aimless without their boss. This was his fight, not theirs. Someone could take his place now—and that was probably more important.

They got me into the back seat with Laura, and Bleu drove us to the hospital.

"Stay with me, okay?" Laura kept slapping my cheek to keep me awake.

"Sweetheart...I'm not going to make it."

"Yes, you are." She stripped off pieces of her own shirt and tied them around my body, stanching a wound that had already bled too much. "Stay with me."

"Look at me."

She continued to apply pressure, but her eyes locked on to mine.

"I love you."

Her eyes started to water.

I wanted to say more, but then the world went black.

The first thing I noticed was the heat on my face.

Warmth of sunshine.

I moved my fingers and felt the softness of sheets.

Then I felt fingers that weren't mine.

"Bartholomew?" Quiet. Desperate. Gentle.

My eyelids were heavy. It took two attempts to get them open. Then the world was blurry. It took several blinks to focus on the woman holding a vigil at my bedside. Once my eyes found hers, she squeezed my fingertips. "Sweetheart?" My voice was hoarse, like my vocal cords had been cut then regrown.

"Yes, I'm here."

We sat like that for a while, and all the events that had led up to this moment slowly came back to me. "I survived."

"Of course you did. You had internal bleeding from a few organs, but they were able to fix everything and give you a blood transfusion. You were in critical condition for a while, but then you eventually stabilized."

I replayed the moment Leonardo went down. A bullet through the head. His brains all over my apartment floor. "I'm sorry about your father."

Her expression didn't change, and she didn't say anything. It was silent, a complexity of emotions on her face. "I made the right choice."

"It's a choice you shouldn't have had to make."

She focused her gaze on our locked fingers.

"When can I leave?"

"Not for a few days."

I let out an annoyed sigh when I shouldn't, not when I should just be grateful to be alive.

"There's someone else who wants to see you." She released my hand and walked out of the room.

A moment later, Benton walked inside, his eyes devoid of the concern Laura possessed. He stopped at the bedside, hands in his pockets, looking at me with those crystal-blue eyes. Laura shut the door to give us privacy.

Nothing was said.

We just stared at each other.

Benton eventually took a seat.

"Bleu told you?"

He gave a nod.

"He made the right decision." I would have preferred to die than let anything come near Benton, Constance, and their children.

"How did Leonardo know about us?"

"I don't know. I'm guessing Silas had something to do with all this before he died."

Benton focused his gaze out the window.

"I'm sorry."

He didn't accept the apology. "Maybe it's time to move on."

I stared at the side of his face, thinking about our partnership before Claire had taken him away from me. It was fun—in its own way. The streets were stained with our dominion, and men feared us the moment we stepped into a room. He'd been the only man I'd wanted to share my power with. "Yeah...maybe it is."

After a few days, I was finally discharged from the hospital.

Bleu and Laura took me home. They tried to get me into a wheelchair, and when they didn't stop pestering me about it, I broke that piece of garbage. After that, they didn't ask me again.

I made it into my apartment, which had been cleaned so thoroughly I didn't notice any evidence of bloodshed. The rug in the entryway had been replaced with a brand-new identical one, and the table had been returned to its rightful place. My butler was there to greet me, looking me over like I'd aged a decade.

I walked into my home straight and tall, but every move I made hurt like a bitch. I was sick of that goddamn hospital bed and the way it made me look weak, so I was done with that bullshit.

Laura came to my side. "Do you have a bedroom downstairs?"

I gave her the coldest look.

"You don't want to walk up and down the stairs every day—"

"I'm fine." I moved to the stairs and walked up normally, making my way to the upper floors.

Down below, I heard Bleu speak. "He's a bit stubborn."

"A bit?" Laura snapped.

I made it into my bedroom. The curtains were already closed like my butler had assumed I would head straight to bed. The wet bar called my name, but with all the shit I was on, I knew that would be a recipe for suicide.

Laura stepped into my room a moment later.

I headed into the bathroom and started the shower. It'd been days since I'd been allowed a proper shower. My beard was scruffy and uncomfortable, and my skin was oily. The second I stepped under the warm water and felt everything wash away, I felt better.

I looked through the glass for Laura, wondering if she would join me.

She wasn't in the bathroom.

I scrubbed myself clean, got the oil out of my hair, and shaved the beard clean off my face. The gauze around my body took up my entire torso, like a boa constrictor wrapping its coils around me.

When I returned to the bedroom, Laura was sitting at the dining table where a tray had been placed. The silver lids were on top of the food to keep everything warm. She didn't look at me even though I was naked. Didn't watch me pull on my boxers and sweatpants. "Get in bed."

"I've been in bed for four days."

"Well, I have a tray for you."

I moved to the dining table and sat across from her. "I don't eat in bed."

"You need to rest—"

"I'm fine." I pulled the tray toward me and removed the lid. No more hospital food—thank fuck.

She watched me eat, having nothing for herself.

"You aren't hungry?"

She shook her head.

I ate in silence, her eyes barely on me. She was there for me, but it seemed like she didn't want to be in the room.

When I finished, I stared at her.

Her mind seemed to be elsewhere because she didn't notice my stare.

"I'm sorry about your father."

"You already said that." She looked at me, her eyes dead.

"Because I am sorry." I'd wanted her to pick me over her father, but not in that scenario.

"I have no regrets, so don't feel sorry."

I studied her face, seeing a woman deeply disturbed.

"If you aren't going to rest or accept my help...then I should go."

Her hands moved to the armrests, and she prepared to rise from the chair.

"Sweetheart."

She stilled at the tenderness in my voice.

"I'm done."

Her features didn't change at all. She either didn't understand—or didn't care.

"I'm ready to walk away from that life."

Indifference was bright in her eyes. "I'm glad that you're ready to move on. You deserve more out of life than crime and bloodshed." She rose from the chair then came to me, like she might kiss me, but there was no passion in her eyes. She leaned down and kissed me on the cheek—and then walked out.

Days passed.

I spent time at home, slowly recovering, getting better every single day.

She didn't call. She didn't text.

After all that…we'd gone right back to what we were.

There was no chance she didn't understand my intentions. She simply didn't want me.

Was there someone else?

It hurt. It hurt a lot more than being stabbed.

I was a proud man, and if I was ever rejected, I took it without objection. Didn't pine. Didn't beg. Just accepted defeat with my head held high.

But I couldn't accept this—not without an explanation.

So I went to her apartment, the nice one I'd bought her, and knocked on the door. I'd stopped surveilling her a long time ago, knowing she had the right to live her life without my intrusion, so I didn't know if she was home. I didn't know where she slept at night. I didn't know if a man would open the door.

Thankfully, it was her.

She was barefoot, in jeans and a top. She wore the same look as the last time I saw her, not the least bit happy to see me.

We stared at each other for a long time, the threshold between us.

I broke the silence. "Can I come in?"

"Yeah...sure." She moved out of the way.

I stepped into her apartment, tones of gray, black, and white. A classy place that only the rich could ever attain.

I moved into the living room, which had floor-to-ceiling windows that showed the city below.

She followed me, arms crossed over her chest. "How are you feeling?"

"Fine." The pain of my wound didn't compare to the pain I felt when she walked out.

Cold. Distant. Empty. That's all she was.

"Do you regret your decision?"

Her eyes lifted and found mine, narrowing in silent protest.

"Because it seems like you want nothing to do with me." It hurt to say those words out loud, because I was afraid she would agree. She should have let her father kill me. She couldn't carry the guilt of her actions. She couldn't look at me and not hate herself.

"Of course I don't."

"Then why?"

"Why what?"

"Why don't you want me?"

She didn't say anything.

I gave her more time, but nothing was forthcoming.

"Is there someone else?" I didn't want to imagine it. Some other man having my woman because I was too late.

"No."

"Are you lying?" The question tumbled out, more aggressive than I intended.

Her eyes widened at my ferocity. "No."

It didn't make any sense. "I said I would walk away from everything. That's what you wanted."

"That was before."

"Before what?"

She didn't speak.

"*Before what?*" I repeated, raising my voice.

"You're only doing this because of what happened to you. If this hadn't happened, we wouldn't have seen each other again."

"You think I haven't been miserable without you every fucking day? You think I've forgotten you while buried in someone else? I've been drinking to forget, but no amount of scotch, gin, or vodka can make me forget you. I've been celibate, because a woman would only make me miss you more, not less. This conversation would have taken place, regardless of what happened."

"But it didn't take place after what happened to me..."

I stared.

"That wasn't enough. I had to shoot my father and save your life to change your mind."

"You didn't change my mind. I've just come to realize my retirement is inevitable. My love for you is inevitable."

Her arms remained locked across her chest.

"Sweetheart, I'm sorry it took so long for me to get here, but I'm here now."

She wouldn't look at me.

"Laura."

"The answer is no."

It was like another knife between my ribs. Nothing I said mattered. Her decision was ironclad. "You ran down there, shot your own father to save my life, put a gun to your ex's head…and you don't want to be with me? Explain to me how that makes sense."

She didn't explain anything.

"I'm giving you what you want. A quiet life. A safe one."

Her eyes found mine again, and then she shook her head. "No."

"No, what?"

"I was willing to sacrifice my dream, but you weren't willing to sacrifice yours."

"What did I just fucking say?" My temper reared its ugly head. This union should be beautiful. We should be fucking on the couch right now. "I'm making the sacrifice to be with you."

"And what if I don't want to make the sacrifice anymore?"

All the anger left my body.

"I want a family, Bartholomew. You didn't make your sacrifice, so I won't make mine. Take it or leave it." Her eyes turned guarded, and she kept the distance between us.

I didn't know what to say, and that showed in the long stretch of silence. "What's wrong with it being just the two of us?"

"Because I want *more*. I want us to make something together. I want to look at my son and see your face. I want to have my children when you're gone."

I'd been so fucking close, and now it slipped away again. "That's not what we agreed to—"

"We agreed you wouldn't give up anything and I would give up everything. That's what we agreed to. Just to refresh your memory."

"And now I'm making a sacrifice—"

"I love you, but it's not enough."

Why did I have to fall for a woman so innately incompatible? I could have any woman in the fucking world, but she had to be the one I wanted. I forced my voice to be calm, and I restrained my anger. "Laura, my parents dumped me in an orphanage. Then a couple years later, they started their family. Not once did they come to find me."

"I know, Bartholomew. And I'm so sorry about that."

"I don't know how to be in a family. I don't know how to be a father. How could I ever know when I didn't have a father of my own? How could I know when I never had the chance to be a regular kid? And you think I'm gonna be father of the year?"

"I can teach you these things."

"I probably won't want them, just the way my father didn't want me."

"That's not true—"

"They never came back for me. It's like I never happened. Abandoned me in that fucking orphanage while they lived just five blocks away. If that's not hate, I don't know what is. Sometimes I still think about killing them..."

Her eyes softened. "I'm so sorry."

"I don't want your goddamn pity. I just want you to understand how deeply I hate kids."

"You don't hate them."

"Yes, I do—"

"You're scared of them. There's a difference."

"Laura, if having kids is that important to you, more important than the love we have for each other, then I'm the absolute worst choice. You should forget about me and find a man who wants what you want instead of forcing me to be something I'm not."

"I know you can do it—"

"It's a twenty-year commitment. It's not going to university for four years then having a great job. It's twenty fucking years. By the time they move out, we'll be old. Too old to live our lives."

"But we'll be living our lives *with* them. The best years of our lives."

"The answer is no."

"Then what will you be doing with your time? We can't travel the world all the time for twenty years. That'll get old. We'll want different things as we age, and having a family is something you'll appreciate—"

"*I said no.*"

Her arms tightened over her chest as her eyes watered. She took a deep breath and blinked, fighting the tears that sprang to the surface.

We were back to the same ending. All roads led us here.

If I hadn't walked into that goddamn shop that afternoon, none of this would have happened.

I wouldn't have loved another woman and lost her.

"Then this is goodbye…"

Again. "Yeah."

"Take care of yourself, Bartholomew."

There were other things I wanted to say, but that would just make it harder on both of us. "I hope you find everything you're looking for…"

26

BARTHOLOMEW

The wrap finally came off—and I had a nasty scar all the way up my torso.

My body had been untouched except the bullet wound Benton had given me. But then I got that cut on my arm from Silas. And now this.

Might have to start covering everything with ink.

I took a drink then returned it to the counter.

"Should you be drinking that?" Benton took the stool beside me.

"I'm off the pain meds."

"So you're feeling better."

"No. I just need a drink more than a pill."

"How's retirement treating you?"

I slouched on the counter as I looked at him. "Is that your way of addressing the elephant in the room?"

Benton ignored the question and ordered a drink.

"Laura and I are done—for good. So I didn't see the point."

"What happened? She shot her father for you."

"Bullshit, that's what happened."

It took Benton a moment to draw the conclusion. "Kids."

"She won't change her mind."

"She changed her mind before."

"Not anymore." I hated it, but I also respected it. She shouldn't be with a man who refused to give her what she wanted. I wasn't worth it. No one was.

"Then why don't you change your mind?"

I raised my glass and clinked it against his. "Good one."

"I'm serious, Bartholomew."

"Are we really going to have this conversation again?"

"Kids aren't hard—"

"They keep you up all night, wake you up at the crack of dawn, are entitled little assholes that don't appreciate a damn thing, and suck the life out of you for twenty years. That's not hard?"

"Even if that were true, there's a lot more to it."

"I argued about this with Laura for an hour. I'm not doing it again."

"Fine." Benton took a drink. "Then lose the love of your life. Fuck whores until she forgets about you and marries someone else. Let her move forward in her life while your life stays exactly the same—except your age."

It took a solid month for me to feel normal again.

The bruises finally faded, and my skin returned to its normal color. It didn't ache every time I moved. I was back in the swing of things. I'd killed off all the men who'd staged that coup with Leonardo and was looking for new recruits to replace them.

Things felt normal again.

Except for one thing...the big hole in my heart.

It got better, but not by much.

I replayed our last conversation over and over and wished it had had a different outcome. I wished I were a different man so I could be with her. I wished she were a different woman, a woman who didn't want a family.

But none of those wishes were reality.

I had my guys watch her apartment again, waiting for the moment she started to see someone else. I hadn't been with anyone since our first breakup, and I continued to hold out just in case anything changed. I guessed there was a part of me that still hoped that it wasn't over...that she would still be mine.

But once a guy slept over, I knew that would be my cue to move on.

I was in my apartment when one of the guys called. They never called because there was nothing to report. She just went to work then went home, alone. So that meant there had been a change in her behavior.

I already knew what he was going to say, but I picked up the phone anyway. "Yeah?"

"Laura has been getting a lot of deliveries."

My eyebrows rose at the odd update. "You called to tell me she's getting shit delivered from Amazon?"

"It's big stuff. Furniture."

Furniture? "What kind of furniture?"

He fumbled in the background, searching through photos. "Crib. Changing table. Rocking chair."

I almost dropped the phone.

"Sir?"

I hung up.

My doctor, Maurice, pulled up the records then slid the laptop across the table toward me. "She had her first appointment with the obstetrician last week. According to the lab reports, she's about two and a half months along."

Nearly three months.

She was almost done with the first trimester.

How long had she known?

"What's the date on this lab report?"

"About six weeks."

She'd known when she killed her father. Had known two weeks before that. Carried this secret alone and never told me.

Benton opened his front door. "What the fuck are you doing here?"

"I need to talk to you."

"Then call."

"I did. You didn't answer."

"Because I'm busy—"

"I need to talk to you. It's important."

Benton looked at me furiously before he shut the door in my face. He was gone for a while before he opened the door and walked out with me. "What is it?"

"Laura's pregnant."

Benton stopped in the middle of the sidewalk.

That was the first time I'd said it out loud—and it was painful.

"Is she with another guy?"

I shook my head.

"So, it's yours."

"Yeah…it's mine." I knew I'd been the only man in her life since we met. "That last conversation we had makes sense now. She wouldn't agree not to have kids…because she was already having a kid."

Benton studied my face. "She wanted to know how you really felt."

I closed my eyes, thinking about all the horrible shit I'd said while my kid was growing in her body at that very moment. "I can't believe she didn't tell me."

"She gave you an out. Gave you a chance to walk away without feeling guilty about it."

"She must have known I'd figure it out eventually."

"But you could always pretend that you hadn't. Could ignore it. Never have a conversation about it."

"I told her if we ever had a kid I wouldn't spend a single moment with it…"

Benton was as hard as I was, and even he raised his eyebrows slightly. "Then she did you a favor, Bartholomew."

"I guess she did…" I stared down the street, spinning in free fall even though my feet were firmly rooted to the ground.

Benton continued to watch me. "Now you can really move on from her."

Could I?

Benton slid his hands into his pockets as he stared at my profile.

"What the fuck do I do?"

"Move on."

"I can't do that to her." Could I really abandon my child the way my father had abandoned me? Could I let her be a single mother?

"I don't think you have a choice now."

I looked at him head on.

"You made it very clear what you want, Bartholomew. She'll know you're only doing it because she's pregnant—and that's not what she wants."

"Then I'll convince her otherwise."

"You'd be lying."

If I abandoned her, she'd be on her own, juggling work and childcare. She might meet someone else, and that man would be a stepfather to my child. Probably wouldn't love them the way he would love his own kids. My kid would always be second best—because I'd chosen to be a coward. "No...I wouldn't be."

27

LAURA

I sat on the floor in the spare bedroom, trying to put the stupid wooden crib together. It came with a diagram and a bunch of screws, but nothing made sense. Every time I put two pieces together, it immediately came apart.

I got so angry I threw the tiny screwdriver at the wall. "Stupid motherfucker..." Couldn't the baby just sleep with me?

Someone knocked on my door. It was faint, coming from the front door and down the hallway. I wasn't expecting company, and all my deliveries were collected by the guys downstairs. I made it to the front door and checked the peephole.

Bartholomew.

Oh Jesus. I stepped back with my hand over my mouth, never expecting to see him again. Why was he there? What did he want?

"Laura?" His deep voice came through the solid wood.

Shit. "I just need a second…" I threw on a sweater even though it was early fall, and I tossed all the baby stuff into the spare bedroom. I shut the door so he wouldn't be able to take a peek.

Then I opened the door, visibly flustered, and came face-to-face with the man I hadn't stopped thinking about since the last time I saw him. He was still tall. Still handsome. Still hard as steel.

We stared at each other, and I wondered what he thought about me. I'd gained some weight with the pregnancy. Not a ton, but enough to make my face fuller, my thighs thicker. The sweater would hide the small bulge.

He continued to stare, looking at me like nothing had changed. "Can I come in?"

I always forgot to invite him in. Whenever I looked at him, I was glued in place. "Yeah." I let him inside, and then we stood together in my big apartment, an apartment far too big for a single person. But I wouldn't be a single person for long.

He took a quick look around then faced me again.

My heart gave out every time our eyes connected. "How's your…?" I gestured to his torso, where he would carry a nasty scar for the rest of his life.

"I don't feel it anymore."

"That's good."

"How are you?"

"Fine." All my priorities had changed the moment I knew I wouldn't be alone anymore. Nothing else seemed important except getting ready for the little person who would share every moment of my life with me. When Bartholomew had told me he still hated kids, I was devastated, and I'd sobbed when he walked out of my apartment. His rejection had hit me differently when I'd already felt the life growing inside me, a life he would never know. "You?"

"You already asked me."

"I mean…with work…Benton."

"It's fine."

Now we'd run out of things to talk about. "Did you come here for a reason…?"

His eyes burned into mine, deep and powerful, claiming me as his even though I hadn't been his in a long time. "I came here for you. I want us to be together. This time apart…I can't do it anymore."

I saw the sincerity in his eyes, saw the man of my dreams pining for me, but instead of making me feel good, it felt like torture. "Nothing has changed."

"I want to be with you—whatever your terms may be."

My eyes flicked back and forth, excited but also confused. "I…I don't understand."

"What don't you understand?"

"You just…changed your mind?"

"I realized any life with you is better than the one I have by myself."

"But you don't want kids. You made that very clear."

He stared at me for a while, not blinking. "I feel differently now."

"Why?"

"Because I do."

Something didn't feel right. It was too easy. "You told me you *hate* kids."

"And you made me realize I'm just scared of them—"

"You told me if we ever had a kid, you wouldn't even be there when they were born—"

"*Laura.*" He winced when I repeated his words. "I remember what I said. You don't need to remind me. I don't want that to be the reason we aren't together. Whenever that time comes in our lives, I'll do my best to be ready for it, to be the best father I can be. I'm willing to try for you."

It still didn't feel right. Never once had Bartholomew ever even remotely entertained the idea, and now here he was, with a complete change of heart. I studied his face, searched for answers in his eyes, his expression, but I didn't find anything.

But then...it hit me.

The reason he'd shown up at my apartment out of the blue...was because he knew.

He knew. "No..."

"What?"

"This is not how I wanted it to be."

His eyes narrowed and his face hardened.

"This is not the love story I want…"

"Laura—"

"Get out."

"I'm not leaving. Not this time. Not ever."

"I gave you the opportunity to choose me for love, not obligation. You made that choice, and now you have to stick with it."

"I'm not here out of obligation—"

"Yes, you are. That's the only reason you came to my front door."

"Laura, I could have just gone about my life without a care. I didn't have to come here. I didn't have to care. But I'm here because I do care, because I don't want my kid to have a stepfather, because I don't want my kid to know what it's like to know their father doesn't give a shit whether they're dead or alive."

I stepped back, my privacy violated, my world upended.

"Sweetheart—"

"No. I know how you really feel."

"And those feelings changed the instant I knew," he snapped. "That's how it works, right? You aren't ready to be a parent until you're forced to be a parent. You don't know how it really feels to have a kid until that moment is upon you. I know how I feel now. I want to do this with you."

My arms crossed over my chest, and I stepped back.

"You know what I said to Benton when he was having a kid?"

"You told him to get her an abortion."

"Which is an option for us since we're still in the first trimester."

My eyes narrowed on his face.

"Have I said that?"

"Because you know I would say no."

"I have no idea how you feel about this, Laura. Because we haven't talked about it. Because you didn't tell me. And no, I haven't suggested it because I would never let anything happen to our son or daughter. How can I hate something that's half you?"

I looked away.

"Laura—"

"You say this now, but you'll leave eventually... You'll leave when things get hard. And I can't deal with that. I'd rather you not be a part of this than watch you abandon us later."

He cocked his head slightly as he stared at me.

The stare was so intense I looked away.

"When have I not been loyal to you?"

I kept my eyes on the floor.

"I sacrificed everything for you, Laura. I let my men die for you. When Silas came for you, I killed him and all the rest. When this relationship failed, I bought you this apartment so you'd never have to sleep in that tainted place. I've *always* been loyal to you. And I will remain loyal to you through this."

"I don't want loyalty, Bartholomew. I want us to be in love—"

"We are in love."

"And we're growing our family...and we're so excited for it. I don't want the man I love to come back because he has to. I don't want a promise he'll stay...because if we were happy, that promise wouldn't need to be made in the first place."

He turned quiet.

"I just...don't want it to be this way."

He stayed quiet.

I looked at him, seeing his focused stare.

"No, it's not in the way that you described, but I think it's more profound. If it weren't, I wouldn't be here right now. The second I knew, all those misgivings and fears vanished. I knew I was fully invested in this. I knew I wanted to be with you every day for the rest of my life. I knew I wanted to be the father to this kid, not someone else. All my priorities changed in an instant. I think that's a better story than the one you imagined."

"I...I don't know." My arms remained locked across my chest, like that would somehow protect my heart.

"You don't have a choice, Laura. I'm here. End of story."

"Yes, I have a choice—"

"Do you think I'll be a bad father?"

The question made me hesitate. "I-I didn't say that."

"Then why the hesitation? Why the resistance?" His eyes were slightly angry, filled with smoke.

"As I already said—"

"I love you, Laura. I want to be with you. I want to raise this child with you. Why can't you just accept that?"

Now I was at a loss for words.

"It's because you think I'll fail. It's because you think I'll be a shitty dad—"

"I don't think that, Bartholomew."

"I'm not good enough for you—"

"No!"

"Then for fuck's sake, be with me." He stared me down, breathing hard, his eyes wide with anger.

I ran out of reasons. I ran out of excuses. He'd broken through all the barriers that protected my heart. "Okay..."

The moment his mouth was on mine, I was taken to a different place.

It was familiar. Warm. Inviting. Safe.

His big hand cupped my entire neck as he kissed me, his strong mouth devouring mine with romantic aggression. His hand squeezed my ass just the way he used to, and he didn't hesitate when he had more to grab.

My hand cupped his hard cheek, feeling the harsh prickle of his jawline. When my lips parted, he breathed new life into me. He filled my lungs with love, with desire. When we were reunited, our spark kindled and we burst into flame, burning away all the heartache that had happened between us.

When my hand glided up his shirt to feel his bare skin, he yanked the garment over his head and tossed it aside. Only a single second passed before our lips were locked again. His hand gripped my cheeks harder as he guided me back toward the bed.

The clothes dropped quickly. His clothes and boots were in a pile, and my jeans and socks sat right on top. His hands slid underneath my sweater and started to remove it.

My hands steadied his automatically.

His eyes locked on mine.

I wasn't sure why I did it. Insecurity. Fear. "I'm not the way you remember..."

His confident eyes burned into mine without hesitation. Then he moved his hand to his torso, to the hideous scar that blemished his beautiful body. "Neither am I, sweetheart." His hand went back underneath my sweater, and he pulled it over my head. He took the shirt underneath with it, revealing my naked body, my slightly bigger tits.

Now I was on display—and I was scared.

He looked down at me, looking at the body that had already changed in subtle ways. My stomach was a little bit distended, easy to hide in clothes but not easy to hide in my bare skin. Fully naked, I knew every difference was obvious. I'd accepted the changes in my body, the ones that would come in the future, but I knew it was different for him. All these changes were warnings—warnings of the baby to come.

His big hand pressed to my stomach, his longer fingers spanning the entire area, his thumb reaching the valley between my tits. He left it there, like he expected a heartbeat or a kick. Then his eyes lifted to mine, the smolder deep in his gaze, like he wanted me and wanted me now.

He placed me on the bed and moved on top of me.

My heart raced with excitement because I'd imagined this moment in the privacy of my home, my fingers deep inside my panties, the lights off so no one could see my indiscretion from the building across the street.

He positioned one of my thighs against his chest as he bent me underneath him. He drew closer and locked his eyes on me as he guided himself to my entrance.

I was so hot. So desperate. So ready to feel this man inside me once more.

I felt him give a gentle push against me. Then another. On the third try, he slid inside, sheathed by the wetness that was so plentiful it was almost embarrassing. He sank all the way inside, burrowing into me like a bear about to hibernate for the winter. A little moan escaped his sexy mouth, and he looked at me with raw possession.

It felt so good, and nothing had happened yet.

He started to move, started to rock nice and slow, to take a moment for us to enjoy how well our slick bodies fit together. His breaths grew short and shallow instantly, and I writhed as my sharp nails scratched at his skin.

He struggled to make love the way he did before, because he hit his threshold in record time. He had to pause before he could go again, just because it felt that damn good.

I was so turned on by this man that I didn't need much to come. Just having him inside me, having him in my body and my heart, was enough to make me slip away. My hand cupped his face as I felt my body tighten into a long, drawn-out explosion. "I love you…" I was on fire. I was tight. I was free. Tears sprang to my eyes, and I rocked into him as the most exquisite pleasure overtook my body.

He watched me come, giving me quicker strokes to make me finish on a high. He breathed hard as he struggled, but he was determined to please me before himself. He watched the production as he rocked into me harder, waiting for the tears to slide down my cheeks before he finished himself. "I love you."

There was no talking for the rest of the evening. We rested beside each other, his hand on my stomach, and then we started up again. I was on top, straddling him as he leaned against the headboard, and then he took me from behind, his hand fisting my hair like a lasso. We were back in time, fucking in a hotel room, living in the moment because there was no future.

Except we did have a future. A long one.

I fell asleep beside him, and when I opened my eyes, he wasn't there.

It was dark outside.

When I felt the sheets, they were cold.

I felt a jolt of fear, like he'd walked out of my life for good, but then I told myself that was nonsense. Half asleep, I was still partially in the land of dreams. I got out of bed and found that his boots were still on the rug.

I went to search for him, and when I heard a noise coming from the baby's room, I knew that was where he'd gone. I rounded the corner and looked inside, seeing him putting the crib together. It was nearly done, and he finished a couple of the remaining screws before he tested it by shaking it, making sure nothing came loose.

I leaned against the doorframe and watched him, arms across my chest, seeing him in a whole new light.

He stared at the crib for a while before he looked at the other things I'd bought. The changing table was still in the box. There were diapers, a couple of toys, a breast pump, things I'd ordered online.

"Thank you."

He slowly turned around to look at me. It wasn't clear whether he'd known I was there or not. His dark eyes looked at me, seeing me standing there in nothing but a shirt and panties. "Do cribs come in black?"

I grinned because I knew he was serious.

He smiled back.

"What if it's a girl?"

"Girls like black." He set down the tools then came to me in the hallway. "Black goes better with my apartment anyway."

"Your apartment?" I asked.

"I assumed that's where we would live."

I stared at him for a while before I walked into the living room. This was a beautiful place, but it'd been far too big for me, making me feel lonelier than I would have in a smaller place. "I hadn't thought about it." I hadn't thought about anything except fucking since he'd walked in the door.

"Think about it now."

"It seems a bit much. I mean, do we need a butler and staff?"

"Yes."

"I don't want our child to be spoiled."

"That's why we teach them how to be rich. Believe it or not, it's not for everyone."

This was so weird. Bartholomew and I were having a discussion about raising kids. Well, a disagreement about raising kids. "I like this apartment."

He took a quick scan of it. "It's small."

"*Small?*" It was at least three thousand square feet.

"Kids run around, don't they?"

"Yes, but they don't train for marathons in the house."

A subtle smile moved on to his lips. "We don't have to decide this now."

"Well...you think it's smart to continue to live there? Shouldn't you start over somewhere else?" Anyone who wanted him dead would know exactly where he slept at night. Where we all slept at night.

He considered the question in silence. "Once I step down, I have no power, and once I have no power, I become useless. Why attack a useless man?"

"I don't know… Revenge?"

His eyes were locked on mine, studying my face. "I find it unlikely someone would harbor a grudge that long, that they would wait for me to retire before provoking me. We'll continue to have security around us, regardless."

"Like, forever?"

"Yes. Forever."

"Then you are concerned."

"Cautious is the word you're looking for. Anyone who has substantial assets has a private security team. You can be a nobody, but if you have money, you're always a target."

"Well…I want a life of peace and quiet."

"It will be peaceful. It will be quiet. I'll worry about these things so you don't have to."

Now that I was going to be a mother, I would probably worry every day for the rest of my life. "Are you set on living in Paris?"

His eyes shifted back and forth between mine. "I'm set on being with you—wherever we are."

"Then maybe we should start a new life somewhere else."

He considered the suggestion in silence. "Where would you like to go?"

"I don't know...Florence?"

His face remained hard.

"I've always loved it there. My sister is there. I think it'd be a nice place to start a life."

The silence continued.

"Unless you have another place in mind?"

He never answered the question. "All my assets are here in France. I'll have to travel from time to time to manage my businesses."

"Oh..." I hadn't thought of that.

"As long as that's acceptable to you, then that's fine with me."

"Really?"

"There's nothing else to keep me here."

"There's Benton."

"I'll see him when I stop by. He's also busy with his family, as I'll be."

He continued to watch me, seeing the thoughts move across my mind.

"What?"

"I'm waiting for further demands."

"They aren't demands, Bartholomew. They're compromises."

"Is there anything else?"

"When are you going to leave the Chasseurs?"

He turned quiet again. "I'll need a week. It's not something I can just walk away from without explanation."

"I understand."

We stared at each other.

"It'll be weird…when you're awake during the day."

That subtle smile was there again. "We're having a baby, sweetheart. I think I'll be up all night as usual."

28

BARTHOLOMEW

I sat on the throne made of skulls, the men talking around me, the air stale this deep underground. Ten years of my life had been spent there. Only one friendship had been made, but a lifetime of loyalty had been forged with many.

Without it...I wasn't sure who I was anymore.

Just a man.

A father.

A husband...someday.

I couldn't lie and pretend this was easy, to forsake my entire identity, all I'd ever known. But it was the price I had to pay to have what I wanted, to keep my family safe.

I waited at the bar.

He walked inside, fifteen minutes late.

When I noticed the stain on his shirt, I assumed his newborn had stalled him.

That was going to be me soon enough.

Benton sat beside me, ordered his drink, and then looked at me.

"We're moving to Florence."

"What's in Florence?"

"A life away from this."

He gave a slight nod. "It's probably for the best."

"It's a little warm for my taste."

"Guess you won't be able to wear black all the time."

I grinned slightly.

"Have you resigned?"

"Not yet. I can't do that until I find someone to replace me."

"I'm not sure if you can be replaced, Bartholomew."

With someone else in charge, the operation would be different. Everything would change. It bothered me, but I had to learn to let it go. "I actually have someone in mind…but I wanted to run it by you."

Benton stilled when I spoke, his fingers freezing on the glass.

"I'll only ask if I have your blessing."

He stared at me, his eyes hard, angry but also calm.

"Otherwise, I'll pick someone else."

"Thanks for putting me on the spot."

"You can say no, Benton. That's all you have to say."

He gave a loud sigh then rubbed the back of his head. "Jesus…"

"I have my answer."

"No…"

I stared down into my drink.

"I don't want to be the reason."

"This could affect you later, Benton."

"I realize that."

"Maybe you should move to Florence, then."

"Doesn't matter where we live." He took a drink. "You really think he's the best choice?"

Other men had been with me longer, since the very beginning. "When everything went to shit, Bleu was loyal to me—to the very end. I can't say the same for the rest of them. Maybe they didn't oppose me, but they didn't mitigate the disloyalty either."

"But do you think he's cut out for the job? Bleu's always been quiet."

"Is quiet a bad thing?"

He shrugged.

"I don't talk when I fuck. I don't talk when I kill. Really, I don't say much at all."

"It sounds like you've thought this through. If that's what you want to do—do it."

I took a drink and let the burn go down my throat. "Speak now or forever hold your peace."

"It's fine, Bartholomew. I think it's a mistake. I think he'll come to regret it. But he has to crash and burn and learn this on his own."

The conversation died, and we drank in silence at the bar. Another round was ordered, and we continued to sit there. I used to pity Benton because his life had ended when he'd had Claire, but now the same had happened to me.

"How are things going with Laura?"

I stared into my glass. "I'm happy to have her back. Whenever we're together...it's always right."

"That's good. And the baby?"

"I know it's real, but I haven't come to accept it's real."

"And it won't feel real until you hold the kid in your arms. No matter how big her belly gets."

Her stomach was different. Her face was different. The changes were subtle, but I'd noticed them the second I looked at her. They didn't bother me at all, and once my hand felt the little bump, I actually liked it. In a sick and twisted way, I enjoyed the fact that I was responsible for all these transformations. "I'm happy to be with Laura, but I'm not happy about all the changes that are about to happen. My life has been exciting, but now it'll be repetitive, monotonous, predictable..."

"Predictable is the last word I would use to describe raising a kid."

"But it's everything else. What will I do with my time?"

"Find a hobby."

"Making money is my hobby."

"Then make money."

"Making money *illegally* is my hobby." I took another drink. "I know this is what Laura wants, but I suspect she'll regret all these changes, seeing me in a light she's never seen me in before. Boring. Fat. Powerless."

"Fat?" he asked. "Do I look fat to you?"

I smirked.

"Not everything has to change, Bartholomew. Some things, but not all things. And she's not going to want you less in this new role."

"We'll see..."

29

LAURA

I hadn't seen Bartholomew much that week.

I spent that time researching homes in Florence, wondering if he wanted to spend our lives in a Tuscan villa outside Florence, or if we wanted to be right in the heart of the hustle and bustle.

He stopped by in the evenings, fucked me in several different ways, and then left again. Our relationship was back to what it used to be, but something was different. He was distant with me, even more distant than he used to be.

I worried he'd had a change of heart. Getting prepared to step down gave him a moment of self-reflection, and he realized it wasn't worth giving up to raise a family. I worried he would walk through that door and say it was all over again.

This silence also made me think of other things.

My father.

I'd been too busy surviving, too busy missing Bartholomew to let the guilt dig underneath my skin. But now it hit me like a sack of bricks to my head. His body had been returned to Florence to be buried beside my mother, not that he deserved it, and I didn't attend the funeral.

As the person who killed him, I thought that seemed highly inappropriate.

I wasn't sure what would happen to the Skull Kings, if someone new had already taken his place. My sister called and said horrific things to me. I could only make out some of the words in her sobs, and they were harsh.

I replayed that moment over and over in my head, wondering if I could have done something else, made a different decision, done something that kept them both alive, but I didn't see any other outcome.

It was my father or Bartholomew.

I'd picked the right man, but it hurt that I had to choose at all.

I'd picked the love of my life. The father of my child. The man I hoped to marry someday.

I was on the couch in the living room when the door opened and he walked inside. It was just like old times, when he came and went without warning or explanation. The second he entered the room, the energy changed, became charged with his immense presence. He was in all black, his leather jacket keeping him warm in the fall evening, and his boots made a distinct sound against the hardwood. He always glanced around when he entered the room before he looked at me.

I was in my sweats because I hadn't expected him that evening. My hair was up in a bun, and I wore a sweater to hide my stomach. I wasn't ashamed of the life growing inside me, but I wasn't ready to admit how drastically my body would change. Like most women, I would probably have permanent stretch marks. Maybe a C-section scar. Permanent imperfections that would mark my passage through motherhood.

He took the seat beside me, the fireplace aglow with the flames, and his hand absent-mindedly moved underneath my sweater to feel the little bump that I tried to hide. His hand was searingly warm, like a hot pan right against my skin.

My hand moved on top of his, and the second the three of us touched, I felt at home. I loved this man in a way I'd never loved anyone in my whole life, and I was so happy we'd made something together, something that would outlast our lifetimes. We would be gone, but our love would live on.

But then I looked into his eyes—and saw nothing there.

"Bartholomew?"

He turned his head farther toward me, showing most of his face.

"I only want you here if you want that too."

His eyes were still as they looked at me. His hand remained pressed into my body. "I come here every night to be with you. My hand rests here to feel the life we made together. So what makes you think I want to be anywhere else?"

"The look in your eyes…"

He stared at me.

"You look sad."

"That's just how I look, sweetheart."

"No, it's not," I said quickly. "Your eyes are empty. You look like...you've lost everything."

He stared at me without breathing, wearing the most strategic poker face I'd ever seen. He completely shut me out, barring access to his complex thoughts and deep emotions.

"Bartholomew..."

He pulled his hand away then sat forward on the couch, giving me his shoulders and back.

Maybe I shouldn't have said anything.

"I asked Bleu to take my place. He agreed. I made the introductions. Briefed him on all our projects. Announced my imminent retirement to the men who have served me these last ten years. I'm not going to lie and pretend this has been easy. I'm not going to lie and pretend I won't miss it sometimes."

"If this isn't what you want—"

"It is. But it doesn't make it easy. I've had nothing my whole life—except this. Without it...I'm nothing."

"That's not true."

He rose from the couch then walked toward the fire so he could stare at it. "I'm no longer the man you fell for. I'm not dangerous. I'm not powerful. I'm not enigmatic. I'm just...me."

I came up behind him, staring at his back. "That's what I want, Bartholomew. That's all I've ever wanted. Just you."

He didn't turn around.

"This baby will change my body. I'll never be the same. But I know you'll still love me."

He turned his head first, and then the rest of his body followed.

My hands moved up his chest until I cupped his cheeks. "I'm so in love with you. Not your money. Not your power. But your heart. Your loyalty. Your eyes. You don't need the Chasseurs... Not when you have me...us."

His eyes were glued to my face. He didn't draw breath. He didn't blink. He stayed that way for a long time, his eyes locked on mine as he gauged my sincerity. Then his arms suddenly circled me, and he pulled me into his chest. His mouth didn't crush against mine. Instead, he hugged me. Rested his chin on my head. And held me in front of the fire.

30

LAURA

I sat on the balcony in my bikini, letting the sun soak into my skin because it was a warm day despite the month. Now my stomach was so protruded, there was no doubt that I was pregnant.

I heard the door open and close from inside the room, so I knew Bartholomew was back.

He took the seat beside me and pulled out a Styrofoam container from a plastic bag. "Riso gelato." He took off the lid and handed me a spoon.

"Thank you." I grinned as I grabbed it from him and took my first bite. "Oh, I missed this. I used to eat this all the time as a kid."

He sat back and watched me. "Then I suspect our kid will too."

"You don't want to try it?"

He shook his head. The man never ate sweets. Didn't touch the basket of bread at dinner. Always had chicken with vegetables for dinner. Basically, he was the most boring man alive.

But he was super sexy, so it was fine.

"The real estate agent called," he said. "There's a new property outside the city."

"Where?"

"Casole d'Elsa."

"That's a beautiful area. Just a bit of a drive from the city. What do you think about living that far away?"

He gave a shrug, sitting in his black jeans and t-shirt. "Whatever you want, sweetheart."

"That didn't answer the question."

He gave a slight smile. "You're the one in charge as far as I'm concerned."

"But you must have an opinion. I want to take your preferences into account."

He looked out over the balcony, the Duomo in the distance. "I don't know shit about kids, so I'll have to defer to your expertise as to what's best for our family. Living in Florence may be ideal when they're older and can walk to school, but perhaps the countryside is best for when they're infants. We can always change our minds later. I'm keeping this place, so it'll always be here when we need it."

I studied the side of his face as I replayed his words in my mind. "They?"

He turned to look at me. "I assumed you'd want more than one."

It was a beautiful villa with olive trees planted around the property. Two stories and expansive, it was far too big for two people. It had a pool, a large lawn, a view of the valley to the west. A long winding path led to the top of the hill where the beautiful home sat, the pathways lined with stone, the walls a Tuscan beige.

It was beautiful.

With my hand on my bump, I walked through the chef's kitchen, the large sitting room, the six bedrooms and eight baths, the outdoor terrace perfect for entertaining under the summer sky.

Bartholomew trailed behind, taking his own path through the home, examining the technical aspects of the house, like the water heater, the furnace, the fireplaces, all the boring stuff that men cared about.

"What do you think?" He joined me in the courtyard, finally wearing something other than black. He wore a white t-shirt and jeans, and the color brought out the richness in his eyes.

"Uh, it's gorgeous. That's what I think."

"You want it, then?"

"I don't know…"

"Your hesitation? It seems like everything is up-to-date. It's turnkey."

"Um, how about the price?"

His eyebrows furrowed. "What about it?"

"It's a lot."

"Is it?"

"Are you being serious?"

"I'm always serious, sweetheart. I'll tell the real estate agent to submit our offer."

"Whoa, hold on." I grabbed his wrist before he walked away. "It's your money. I want to make sure this is something you want—"

"*Our* money."

"Bartholomew, I'm not your wife—"

"You're my woman. Same thing." His deep eyes studied mine. "The price is nothing to me. Let's get it."

"Are you sure?"

"Yes," he said without hesitation. "Come on, let's get our house."

Months later, we moved in to the villa.

I was six months pregnant, entering my final trimester, and I was big and uncomfortable. I was insecure too, and I missed being the petite little thing I used to be. I missed when my tits were smaller, when my favorite jeans fit me perfectly, when my face wasn't so full.

Bartholomew acted like he didn't notice these changes.

God bless that man.

We'd had a designer prepare our home with furniture of Italian craftsmanship. Everything was local, but a couple culinary items were from France, like the stove and pots and pans, at Bartholomew's instance.

By the time we moved in, it was winter, so the sky was overcast and the world was cold. The fireplace was always lit in every room, and the radiant heat kept our feet warm when we walked across the hardwood.

I still struggled to get accustomed to Bartholomew's presence. He used to be gone all night, but now he was right beside me. He was also wide awake during the day, spending his morning in an extensive gym session before he had his morning coffee. He spent his time reading on the couch. Then in the evening before dinner, he worked out a second time, doing his cardio. He was already ripped, but he became even tighter, his muscles more pronounced.

So basically, he got hotter and I got fatter.

It started to wear me down, to make me feel like I didn't deserve him. When people saw us together, they probably wondered what I'd done to land a man like that.

Maybe I'd tricked him into knocking me up so he would have to stay.

He stepped out of the shower with the towel around his waist. He was mostly dry, his hair a little messy from scrubbing the towel through the strands. All the cords on his arms and neck bulged like a tightrope. "Something on your mind?" He opened his dresser drawer and pulled out a pair of boxers before he dropped the towel.

His ass was so tight.

I sat up in bed with a book in my lap. Or, I should say, on my stomach. "No. Why?"

He pulled on his boxers before he tossed the towel in the bin. "You're different."

"Well...I am pregnant."

He walked toward the bed, his authoritative eyes locked on mine.

That was all he had to do to put me on edge, to know that he was dead serious. If he looked at our kids like that, we would never need to put them in time-out.

"Laura, I know there's something on your mind." He pulled back the sheets so he could lie beside me.

"It's nothing."

That angry look returned.

"I'm just feeling a bit self-conscious, okay?"

"Why?"

"*Why?*" I set the book aside then balanced a glass of water on my stomach. "That's why."

His gaze remained cold, like he didn't understand the point I tried to make.

I put it back before I spilled it. "I'm getting fatter every day, and you're getting hotter…something I didn't think was possible."

"I don't have anything else to fill my time, Laura."

My hand moved over my enormous stomach, as if I could somehow hide it underneath my arm. "I'm big. I'm ugly. I'm not the sexy woman who used to meet you in secret hotel rooms…"

"Sweetheart."

I ignored him.

"Look at me."

"No…"

"I fuck you every night like we're still in that hotel room."

"I don't know how."

"Because watching you struggle to carry my child is a turn-on."

I hesitated before I looked at him.

"It's purely biological and animalistic, but it turns me on, nonetheless. And once our baby is born and your body is different, either because it carries scars or stretch marks, those will turn me on too, because of the sacrifice you made."

This man was something else.

"Now get on your hands and knees." He grabbed the sheets and tugged them off my body. "Face down, ass up."

I noticed Bartholomew had spent a lot of his time outside, braving the intense cold like it wasn't a second thought. When I looked through the windows, I saw him on our property, farther down in the valley.

I had no idea what he was doing.

We owned a lot of land, so much of it that there wasn't another house in sight.

He eventually returned in the late afternoon before it got dark. He stripped off his jacket and left it on the coatrack by the front door before he walked inside. Dinner was on the stove, and he took a quick glance to see what was on the menu before he washed his hands in the sink. Then he walked up to me, gave me that look I never saw him give anyone else, and kissed me as he pulled me close, his hand on my ass as always.

I melted on the spot. "So...what were you doing out there?"

"I got an idea."

"Like a gazebo?"

"No. An old acquaintance of mine started a winery to wash his money, but then worked at it full time once he retired from his other profession. Thought I could do the same."

"We're going to have a winery?" I asked in surprise.

"No. Olive oil. We'll have olive groves throughout our property. It'll give me something to do. Something legal.

One day, our children will ask how we have money when we don't work. I'd rather them see me as a hard worker than a lazy enigma."

"They would never think that."

"It'll also give me something to do with them. Something to bond over."

"Yeah, that's nice." I was glad he'd found something to invest his time in, because he'd been a free agent these last few months. I'd expected him to crack at some point, to succumb to the boredom or become resentful toward me. But he never did. "Dinner should be ready, so I'll set the table."

As if he didn't hear what I said, he changed the subject. "I thought we could go into Florence tomorrow."

"Why?"

"I need to grab a few things."

"Alright."

We drove into the city, a thirty-minute drive, and then left the car at his apartment. His staff was still there, having nothing to do when he wasn't in residence. We'd discussed having them come to our Tuscan villa, but we also enjoyed this time alone.

We entered his bedroom on the top floor, and that was when I saw the white dress laid out on the bed.

I stilled when I saw it, taking a moment to understand exactly what I was looking at.

Bartholomew stayed by the door. "Come downstairs when you're ready."

"Whoa, hold on." I turned around to look at him. "What is this?"

He leaned against the doorframe and crossed his arms over his chest. "I want to be married before the baby gets here."

"That's fine…but you didn't ask me."

He stared at me for a while. "Why would I ask when I already know your answer?"

"Because it's tradition. It's romantic."

"You know I'm not the kind of man to take a knee and profess my undying love."

"Do I even get a ring?"

He grinned slightly. "Yes. I'll show you when we get there."

With me in a beautiful wedding dress that somehow fit me perfectly, we arrived at the church, and Bartholomew walked me inside. White candles were lit, and the priest waited at the front for our arrival.

Bartholomew was dressed in jeans and a t-shirt, but I could never picture him wearing a suit anyway. He wouldn't look right. He took my hand and walked me to the front, and that was when I saw a familiar face.

"Catherine?"

She came to me and immediately embraced me.

We held each other for a long time.

Bartholomew stepped aside to give us our moment.

After our father had died, we didn't speak, other than that one phone call. I'd assumed we would never speak again, not after my betrayal. But here she was, holding me tight like she didn't want to let go.

She pulled back and looked at me head on. "You look beautiful."

"Thanks, Catherine."

"I-I left him."

My eyes searched her face, seeing the pain deep beneath the surface. "I know it hurts right now, but you did the right thing. Where are you staying?"

"Bartholomew opened his home to me. I've been there for a couple weeks now. He said I can live there as long as I want."

I turned to Bartholomew and locked eyes with him.

He had no reaction. Just held my stare.

I looked at my sister again. "Thank you for coming."

"I wouldn't miss it. I'm so happy for you both." She gave me another hug before she let me go.

I returned to Bartholomew, looking at him with new eyes. "Thank you."

His only response was a subtle nod.

I noticed Benton there as well, standing behind Bartholomew as if they'd just finished talking.

With our hands together, we faced the priest and began the ceremony.

He reached into his pocket and withdrew the small box. He opened it and presented the ring before he grabbed my hand and slipped it onto my finger. I didn't really have a chance to look at the ring until it was already on my hand.

It was enormous. A large diamond to mark his territory for everyone to see. Smaller diamonds were in the platinum. It was an elaborate display of wealth, but I knew Bartholomew wanted me to feel like the most valuable thing he owned.

He promised to love me forever and ended his vows with, "I do."

I assumed he didn't want to wear a ring. It wasn't in his nature to wear jewelry, not even a watch, and such a public display of ownership seemed like something he would shun. But he pulled out another box and grabbed the small black band inside. He slipped it on to his own hand, the matte black distinctive and smooth, but also simple and subtle—just like him.

I smiled and promised to love him forever. "I do."

A distant smile moved on to his lips as he looked at me, my hand in his. Then he brought me close and kissed me, and with complete disregard for the priest standing there, as well as my sister, he grabbed my ass—like always.

EPILOGUE
BARTHOLOMEW

After I parked the car, I walked up the gravel to the winery.

It was a quiet Tuesday in the summertime, tourists on the terrace enjoying their wine tasting. Instead of going into the office, I headed to the rear where their storage and bottling buildings were.

Didn't want to deal with the obnoxious son-in-law again.

When I entered the warehouse, I found Cane on the forklift, trying to put a barrel on one of the top racks.

"Easy, easy," Crow said from the bottom. "It's like you've never done this before."

"Shut up," Cane snapped. "The forklift is glitching."

"Forklifts don't glitch, asshole. It's not a computer."

"Just shut your mouth, asshole." He raised it higher and slid the barrel onto the shelf, but something went wrong and it rolled off the edge and shattered on the floor. Wine went everywhere.

Crow was so angry he didn't say a word.

Cane sighed and dragged his hands down his face. "Jesus fucking Christ."

"I told you to let me do it—"

"It's the forklift!"

"Stop blaming other shit on your inadequacy!"

"What the hell is going on?" A woman walked inside, a brunette in jeans and a blouse. "I can hear you two going at it all the way from the terrace." She glanced at me when she saw me standing there but then looked at the guys.

That was when Crow noticed me. His eyes narrowed on my face like he wasn't the least bit happy that I was there. His mood immediately shifted, and he barked an order to the woman I assumed was his wife. "Button, go back to the terrace."

Without hesitation, she obeyed, giving me a look before she walked off.

Crow walked toward me, and Cane hopped off the forklift and joined his brother.

"What the fuck do you want?" Crow got right in my face, a pit bull defending its territory.

I raised my hands in a subtle gesture of surrender. "I thought we would be on better terms after our last project."

"I don't like people showing up unannounced."

"So, do all your customers make appointments?"

He gave me a hard stare. "I'm not in the mood for your punk-ass sarcasm."

Heavy footsteps sounded behind me, and I knew exactly who it was. "Everything alright, Crow?"

Crow never took his eyes off me. "Not sure yet."

I dropped my hands. "That woman you helped a year ago—she's my wife now. We have a son. He's a couple months old. We actually live just a few miles away from here, so I guess we're neighbors."

Crow ignored everything I said. "What do you want?"

"I've traded adrenaline for domestication. Hasn't been easy. There are days when I feel so restless I could explode...but I never tell her. So I decided to focus my energy on something productive—like an olive oil business."

Crow's eyebrows furrowed.

"I planted additional saplings in the spring, and I know it'll take some time for them to come into maturity, but I was hoping you could help me start this business. Perhaps I can learn a few things from the winery, like shipping, production, distribution."

"And why would I help you?" Crow asked.

I gave a shrug. "You always have an ally right down the street. If shit ever goes down, you've got someone to watch your back. I'm sure your life is unremarkable and peaceful, but that's always a reassurance. And if that's not reason enough, I'm a rehabilitated man who wants to support his family honorably. I want to show my children how to live off the land. I want my kids to see me differently than everyone else I've ever met. You, of all people, can understand that."

Crow was a man devoid of all emotion, and there was only one way to pierce his hardness.

Family.

It was the one and only time he had a heart.

"Alright," he said. "I'll teach you."

When I walked into the house, I found Laura and Demetri asleep on the couch. He was on his stomach on her chest, and they seemed to breathe in sync. Her arms still cocooned him, and the sunlight came through the window and warmed them both.

I approached the back of the couch and stared down at the two of them. The house was silent, which was a rarity, and the world outside was quiet. The olive trees were visible in the distance, climbing up the hill until they disappeared on the other side.

I moved to the armchair and sat there, watching them both sleep, the two things that mattered most to me.

I wasn't sure how long that lasted, how long I sat there and watched them, but it must have been an hour before Demetri grew fussy and started to cry.

Before Laura could fully wake up, I took him into my arms and carried him outside, his favorite place to be. I took him into the sunshine as I bobbed him up and down, turning his cries to little giggles.

He smiled at me.

I smiled back.

Laura followed me outside a moment later. "How'd it go?"

"Good. He said he would teach me the ropes."

"That's nice."

"And then one day, I'll be able teach you the ropes, son." I looked at Demetri, who smiled every time I gave him attention.

Laura covered her mouth as she gave a yawn. "Do you mind if I take a nap? He was up all night."

"No problem."

"Thank you." She directed my face to hers and kissed me. "I love you." She patted my chest and walked back to the house.

I watched her go. "I love you too..."

I unlocked the screen and showed him the pictures in the bar.

Benton smiled. "Looks just like you."

"I know he does." I realized it the first time I saw him. Dark hair. Dark eyes. And he was a long kid, which told me he would be tall.

Benton swiped through more photos before he handed back the phone. "That's a good-looking kid."

"I know," I said, a note of pride to my voice.

"How's Laura?"

"Happy. Already talking about the second one."

"You want another one?" he asked.

I gave a nod. "Wouldn't mind it."

"So, you still hate kids?" He grinned, enjoying the taunt.

I took a drink and ignored what he said.

"That's what I thought."

"It was hard in the beginning. Living in a new place. Stepping down at work. Having nothing to do. But it got easier."

"And Demetri gives you a new kind of purpose."

"Yeah…he does."

"How long are you in town?"

"Just for a couple days. Have to manage a few things. I would have brought them with me, but Demetri is so young, it's easier to keep him in one place."

"I understand," he said. "Well, I'm happy for you." He clapped me on the shoulder. "I never imagined you as a husband and father, but now I can't imagine you being anything but."

I sat at the table alone, a cup of coffee in front of me along with some scones I wouldn't eat. My eyes immediately went to them when they walked in the door. There were four of them, a mother and father with two grown kids.

Some of them were married, so they'd brought their spouses along.

They gathered at a table, ordered their coffees and pastries, and soon the table erupted into loud bursts of laughter.

I sat there and watched it all.

A life that could have been mine.

When I looked at my father, I saw features similar to my own, but I had my mother's eyes. They were both tall, so it was hard to tell whose height I'd inherited. Eventually, the waitress brought out a small cake with a single candle in the middle.

They sang happy birthday.

The cake ended up in front of my father.

They all sang, and then he blew out the candles. He turned fifty-five.

Their evening eventually wrapped up, and after presents were opened, they left the table and gathered outside to say their goodbyes. His son and his wife left. Then his daughter walked off.

It was just the two of them.

I left my table and walked outside. They seemed to be waiting for a cab because their apartment was several blocks away. My mother raised her arm to get the attention of a taxi, but he drove right by.

I moved to the edge of sidewalk, raised my hand, and immediately got a cab to pull over. I opened the back door and held it open for them. "You guys take it."

"Oh, that's so nice," my mother said. "But we couldn't."

"Please," I said as I stepped out of the way. "Happy birthday."

My dad smiled when he heard me say that. "Well, thanks."

I stared him down, hoping he would recognize me, that he would recognize his own blood, but he didn't. "No problem, Dad."

He was just about to turn to the cab when he jerked back toward me. Now he stared at me with a mixture of both fear and terror, like the past he'd been evading all his life had finally caught up with him. His breaths deepened and shortened, and his eyes flicked back and forth as he looked at my features.

My mother was frozen too.

My dad finally spoke. "Ryan...?"

"Yes."

Still in disbelief, he just stared, at a loss for words. "I... I'm sorry. I don't know what to say—"

"I've watched you my entire adult life. Watched you interact with your kids. Watched my birthday come and go without any acknowledgment. Watched the life I could have had from across the street."

"We tried to find you—"

"No, you didn't. And that's okay. I don't want to be somewhere I'm unwanted."

My mother grabbed his arm to steady him.

"I'm not going to watch you anymore. I'm not sad about the life I lost. I'm married now. I have a son. I have my own family. I just wanted you to know that I'm here, that what you did was unspeakable, and you're the ones who missed out on a relationship with me. As a father myself, I don't know how you could possibly justify what you did. But none of that matters anymore."

He was still speechless, somber from my cold words. "I-I want you to know how sorry I am. How sorry we both are."

I gave a slight nod. "Yeah…I'm sorry too."

The second I walked in the door, I heard his footsteps.

"Dad!" He rounded the corner and came down the hall to the entryway. He ran as fast as he could on his little legs and dove right into my shins.

I smiled and lifted him into my arms. "Did you take care of your mother while I was gone?"

"Yeah."

"Of course you did." I kissed the side of his head as I walked into the kitchen.

Laura was finished dinner, her stomach slightly distended with our second baby. "Hey, babe." She came to me and kissed me. "How was Paris?"

I brought her close and kissed her on the forehead. "It was fine."

"That's it?" she asked with a laugh. "Just fine?"

"I saw Benton. He's doing well."

"Oh, that's good."

"And I took care of business. That's about it."

"Well, I'm glad you're home." She kissed me again and got back to work in the kitchen.

"Yeah...me too."

Penelope Sky has a brand-new fantasy romance series under her pen name Penelope Barsetti scheduled to release in the fall, but you can get it MONTHS before everyone else. AND you can get all three books in one sitting instead of waiting months between releases.

Yep, you read that right.

There'll be more than just the ebooks, but autographed paperbacks and limited edition hardcopies, along with a podcast interview with Penelope Sky, a virtual book signing, and more!

About the book:

Enemies-to-lovers...to unlikely allies...to frenemies with benefits...10/10 spice.

A horrible plague has swept the world.

Millions are sick. More are dying.

Except me. I'm immune.

I'm the only one well enough to defeat this plague and save my people.

Except one problem...

Kingsnake--King of Vampires--is intent on finding me. Without my people to feed on, he'll die. My blood is the only thing that will keep him alive.

He won't stop until he finds me.

Binds me.

And makes me his.

Click this link to order your set now: **https://www.kickstarter.com/projects/penelopesky/dirty-blood-trilogy**

Here is a snippet of the book:

Larisa

When I woke up, I devoured the dinner tray that had been left under the door. An hour later, another tray was delivered for breakfast, and I ate that too. Like an animal that had nothing to live for except food, I waited for the next delivery and napped in between. There were books on the bookshelf, books that were written by humans, and that made me realize there had been a line of women that had occupied this room long before I did—and had all died since.

Days passed, and Kingsnake didn't come for me.

He went through so much trouble to capture me, but now, he acted like I didn't exist.

I knew that wouldn't last long. He captured me for a reason—and he wanted a return on his investment.

What would I do when he came for me?

My sword and dagger had been taken. All I had were the items in the room with me. I could break down one of the bedposts and slam it into his head. Pick up the armchair and throw it at him. Slam a book on top of his head. But none of those things would kill him—just piss him off.

My thoughts were shattered when I heard the noticeable click of the lock.

Shit.

The door opened and he emerged—but he didn't look the same.

His black armor engraved with serpents no longer covered his body. There was no tunic either. No cloak. In fact, he didn't wear a shirt at all…

All he wore were trousers that seemed to be made of cotton, the kind of attire he wore in the privacy of his bedchambers when his presence wasn't required elsewhere. That made me think it was evening, or rather his evening, which was morning.

Covered in lean muscles underneath tight skin and corded veins, his fair skin was marked with subtle scars. Some on his arms, some on his torso, a couple on his chest. He was ripped, the strong muscles shifting with the slight movements he made. Those slitted eyes were on me, dark like the bark of a tree after a morning rain. The intensity of his stare was a little terrifying because he didn't need to blink—just like his snake.

I stepped back, putting as much distance between us as the bedroom would allow. All I had within reach was the book I'd been reading, so I held it at my side, ready to smash it on his head once he came close enough.

His eyes never left mine. "You must be as tired as I am."

"I'll never be too tired to fight."

He stared at me a moment longer before he shut the door behind him.

The lock clicked, like someone waited on the other side.

A tense silence fell between us. I stared at him. He stared at me.

White-hot fire leapt from his eyes and burned every piece of furniture. It swallowed the room whole.

I gripped the book tighter. "The feeling is mutual..."

His eyes shifted slightly, narrowing just a little more. "Sit."

"No."

He came at me, still looking like a king even though he wore no clothing.

I gripped my book and prepared to strike him in the temple.

But he walked right past me, even turned his back on me, and took a seat at the dining table.

I watched him move, my fingers loosening on the edges of the spine.

He relaxed against the wooden back of the chair, one ankle crossed and resting on the opposite knee. He crossed his arms over his wide chest before he nodded to the chair across from him. "*Sit.*" His tone deepened and his jawline sharpened, like a parent that had officially run out of patience with a child.

"Why?"

"*Because I said so.*"

"You know, if you just treated me with some respect—"

"Respect is earned here in Grayson—not given."

"You haven't earned my respect either, asshole."

The flames rose, burning the entire palace that he called home. He was willing to burn it to the ground as long as I burned too. "I have a proposition for you—if you would sit and listen."

"A deal with a vampire? No thanks..."

His eyes narrowed. "With Kingsnake, King of Vampires and Lord of Darkness."

I rolled my eyes.

His movements were so fast I didn't see them actually happen. His hand seized me, and then I was in the chair, my ass hitting the wood so hard it would leave a bruise. Then he walked back to his chair with a slow grace, like the ordeal never happened. He faced me, arms across his chest, the flames still burning around him. "I have no intention of biting you this evening."

"Oh goodie..."

His eyes narrowed even more. "You're powerless here, and you conduct yourself like you're invincible."

"I am invincible. I'm the only human who's immune to the disease that's claimed the lives of thousands and poisoned the blood of thousands more. You bite the wrong human—and you're dead. I'm the most powerful goddamn person in the world right now." I wasn't stupid—and I wanted to make that abundantly clear.

He was silent, and slowly, the flames around him started to diminish.

"You think I'm a pain in the ass? Honey, you haven't seen the half of it..."

Silent he remained, watching me across the table, the intensity in his stare remaining but the flames settling. "I can offer you the one thing you want more than anything."

"My freedom?"

"Even more than that."

There was nothing I wanted more than to be free of this monster and the other monsters that followed him. "What is that?"

"A cure."

My expression didn't change, but I felt all the muscles in my body automatically tighten. Against my will, my lungs pulled in a deep breath.

"Do I have your attention?" Those angry eyes now shined with arrogance.

Stubborn to my core, I kept my mouth shut.

"We have the same self-interest. The plague has devastated our food source, and your population has been decimated by the sickness. We can find a cure together—if you cooperate."

"Cooperate?"

"Yes."

"And what does *cooperate* mean?"

He tilted his head the other way, his slitted eyes never leaving my face. "I need to taste your blood."

My stomach tightened with disgust.

"It's the only way."

"Right…"

"If I've fed on someone before, I can identify them based on the taste of their blood alone. It's the same way you can identify someone based on the sound of their voice… their scent. I can taste the properties of your blood, and perhaps I can determine what sets you apart from everyone else."

It felt like a trap. "And in the event you succeed, what then?"

"We invent a cure—and give it to your people."

"Just like that?"

"As I've already said, the eradication of this disease is paramount to our survival. It's decimating our population as much as yours."

"That's not true...you have other options."

"Animal blood is a poor substitute. Yes, it keeps us alive, but it also keeps us weak."

I stared, annoyed with his calmness, with the way his deep voice set the tone of this conversation.

"You're the savior your people need."

I broke contact and looked away.

"You can save them all—and you're unwilling to make this sacrifice?"

"I'm not stupid. I know what you're doing."

"Which is?"

I looked at him again. "You're trying to manipulate me."

"Even if that's true, what does it matter?"

"It is true."

He didn't refute it. "An opportunity has been given to us, but you would throw it away because you're afraid?"

"I'm not afraid. Just don't want a leech on my neck. Don't want to strengthen my greatest mortal enemy. I'd rather watch you wither and weaken until you're dust on the wind..."

The corner of his mouth lifted—and he grinned.

"Did you not understand what I said?"

"There are worse things than my kind in this world..."

"Such as?"

"You'll see—someday."

Trepidation filled my heart, an unease that seeped straight into my bones. I wanted to press him for answers, but I would receive none, especially since I'd refused to comply with every single one of his demands.

"When I said your kind enjoy bloodletting, I meant it. Every prey I've ever had has enjoyed my bite. The only pain you feel is the moment my fangs pierce your skin. But then indescribable pleasure sweeps through you, the kind that will make you beg me to keep going, until I've had every single drop."

"I don't believe you."

His stare was still, eyes locked on to mine, like I wasn't even there. "I've never had to force a woman to be my prey."

"Then why don't you get someone else?"

"Humans normally travel to our gates and offer themselves as prey. We've never had to travel to the kingdoms and capture prisoners. The plague has changed everything."

"Why would they do that? Why would anyone in their right mind want to subject themselves to that?"

He gave a subtle shrug. "Several reasons."

"Such as?"

"One, physical desire."

"Desire? Desire to be bit?"

"Desire to be with a vampire in other ways..."

I couldn't sit across from Kingsnake and pretend he wasn't a treat for the eyes, especially when he was shirtless and muscular. The vampire I usually saw him with was the same way, just more muscular. A lot of vampires were good-looking, but Kingsnake was exceptional. "Is that why you're half naked right now? Because that's not going to work on me."

That knowing grin returned. "I find it more comfortable."

"What are the other reasons?"

"Obsession. Some humans worship our kind. Think we're gods. To serve us is a great honor."

I'd heard about these people before. I'd always dismissed them as crazy enthusiasts.

"And the final, more important reason, is the chance to become a vampire themselves."

Death would be preferrable. "None of those sound remotely appealing."

"The chance to live forever isn't remotely appealing to you?"

"No—because it's not living. You don't have a beating heart. Your lungs don't draw air. You have no soul. When your time comes, you'll just be...nothing."

His expression didn't change, as hard as ever, still like stone.

"That doesn't bother you?"

"Why would it bother me when my time will never come?"

"You're that arrogant?"

"Confident. That's the word I would use."

I stared at this creature across from me, a monster that had a beautiful face, a beautiful body, but an enormous void inside his chest. "If I were to cooperate and we did discover a cure for my people...would you let me go?"

Silence. An eternity of it.

I waited, unsure what he was thinking or if he was thinking at all. His face was hard, and his emotions were subdued.

"Every prey I've ever had has fulfilled their use. Their taste grows stale, and soon, I crave something different. Once I've grown bored of your taste, I will release you. What you choose to do at that time is your concern."

"You don't kill your prey when you're finished with them?"

"No. They usually become prey to someone else. Or they leave." He studied my gaze, watched me work out the information he'd just given me. "Contrary to what you've been told, we're not monsters. We don't kill humans unless by accident. We're no different than fisherman. After we've made our catch, we toss it back into the water."

The comparison was a stretch, but I kept my opinion to myself. "You give me your word? You'll let me go?"

He held my gaze for a long time before he gave a subtle nod. "Yes."

I didn't know him well enough to trust his word, but honorable kings kept their promises—and he seemed honorable.

"I can't force you to do this."

My arms crossed over my chest.

"Because if I do, there's a good chance I'll kill you."

When I pictured myself submitting to his bite, I was filled with self-loathing. But if there really was a possibility this could lead to the salvation of my people...it would be selfish to refuse.

"I need you to submit to me completely."

That was an impossible task.

"Can you do that?"

My hands automatically rubbed up and down my arms, fighting the chill that suddenly crept into the room. My entire life, I'd been warned about the horrors of these creatures, and to allow yourself to be bitten…was unspeakable.

"You can trust me, Larisa."

"Trust you how?"

"Trust that I won't kill you." He hadn't moved in the last ten minutes, hadn't even blinked. His snakelike qualities became more apparent the longer I was in his presence. "Trust that you'll enjoy it."

I was horrified that I was actually considering this.

"Will you let me, Larisa?"

My heart had picked up in speed, and the fast rate made me a little sick. My palms were suddenly clammy even though this place was eternally chilly. I suddenly felt hot, like the sun could pierce through the clouds and solid wall. "Yes…I'll let you."

. . .

Click this link to order your set now: **https://www.kickstarter.com/projects/penelopesky/dirty-blood-trilogy**

Printed in Great Britain
by Amazon